J. T. EDSON'S
FLOATING OUTFIT

The toughest bunch of Rebels that ever lost a war, they fought for the South, and then for Texas, as the legendary Floating Outfit of "Ole Devil" Hardin's O.D. Connected ranch.

MARK COUNTER was the best-dressed man in the West: always dressed fit-to-kill. **BELLE BOYD** was as deadly as she was beautiful, with a "Manhattan" model Colt tucked under her long skirts. **THE YSABEL KID** was Comanche fast and Texas tough. And the most famous of them all was **DUSTY FOG**, the ex-cavalryman known as the Rio Hondo Gun Wizard.

J. T. Edson has captured all the excitement and adventure of the raw frontier in this magnificent Western series. Turn the page for a complete list of Berkley Floating Outfit titles.

J. T. EDSON'S
FLOATING OUTFIT
WESTERN ADVENTURES
FROM BERKLEY

THE YSABEL KID
SET TEXAS BACK ON HER FEET
THE HIDE AND TALLOW MEN
TROUBLED RANGE
SIDEWINDER
McGRAW'S INHERITANCE
THE BAD BUNCH
TO ARMS, TO ARMS, IN DIXIE!
HELL IN THE PALO DURO
GO BACK TO HELL
THE SOUTH WILL RISE AGAIN
.44 CALIBER MAN
A HORSE CALLED MOGOLLON
GOODNIGHT'S DREAM
FROM HIDE AND HORN
THE HOODED RIDERS
QUIET TOWN
TRAIL BOSS
WAGONS TO BACKSIGHT
RANGELAND HERCULES
THE HALF BREED
THE WILDCATS
THE FAST GUNS
CUCHILO
A TOWN CALLED YELLOWDOG
THE TROUBLE BUSTERS
THE LAW OF THE GUN
THE PEACEMAKERS

THE RUSHERS
THE QUEST FOR BOWIE'S BLADE
THE FORTUNE HUNTERS
THE TEXAN
THE RIO HONDO KID
RIO GUNS
GUN WIZARD
TRIGGER FAST
RETURN TO BACKSIGHT
THE MAKING OF A LAWMAN
TERROR VALLEY
APACHE RAMPAGE
THE RIO HONDO WAR
THE FLOATING OUTFIT
THE MAN FROM TEXAS
GUNSMOKE THUNDER
THE SMALL TEXAN
THE TOWN TAMERS
GUNS IN THE NIGHT
WHITE INDIANS
WACO'S DEBT
OLD MOCCASINS ON THE TRAIL
THE HARD RIDERS
THE GENTLE GIANT
THE TRIGGER MASTER
THE TEXAS ASSASSIN
THE COLT AND THE SABRE

J.T. Edson

RETURN TO BACKSIGHT

BERKLEY BOOKS, NEW YORK

RETURN TO BACKSIGHT

A Berkley Book / published by arrangement with
Transworld Publishers, Ltd.

PRINTING HISTORY
Brown, Watson edition published 1966
Corgi edition published 1969
Berkley edition / January 1984
Second printing / December 1986

ISBN: 0-425-09397-2

A BERKLEY BOOK ® TM 757,375
Berkley Books are published by The Berkley Publishing Group,
200 Madison Avenue, New York, NY 10016.
The name "BERKLEY" and the stylized "B" with design
are trademarks belonging to Berkley Publishing Corporation.

PRINTED IN THE UNITED STATES OF AMERICA

For W.O.II Sam Perrie, R.A.V.C.,
The Noblest Dog Man of All

RETURN TO BACKSIGHT

CHAPTER ONE

Father Donglar's Scheme

It could not be claimed that everybody in the Arizona Territory Penitentiary favored the scheme put forward by Father Donglar.

"A musical evening for the prisoners," spat out one of the main-gate guards disgustedly. "They'll be having us serve 'em with breakfast in bed next."

"Back East there's a bunch of them college-boy politicians reckon we ought to treat our prisoners kinder," his companion replied. "Make 'em comfortable, don't give 'em any hard work. That way they'll not do anything bad again. Some of that bunch even reckon we shouldn't hang murderers, want it stopping."

"Nobody could be that stupid," growled the first, then a worried expression crept to his face. "Or could they?"

"You'd think not," the second answered. "It'll be God help the world if they do get their way."

Seated behind the desk in his office, the Warden studied his visitor with some interest. Tall, tanned, handsome, with light brown hair and pale blue eyes, the man called Father Donglar made a striking figure in the black clothing of his order. Smiling in a friendly manner, he waited for the Warden to speak.

"You want to bring a show in *here,* Father?" asked the Warden, after glancing at the letter of introduction which lay before him.

"Not exactly a show, Warden," the other replied. "An entertainment. There will be no girls in scanty costumes showing their legs. No comedian making risqué jokes— and don't look so surprised. I do know such things exist."

From the twinkle in Father Donglar's eyes, the Warden decided that, regardless of his cloth, he was not entirely averse to seeing the kind of show he mentioned. Clearly the Father took a broader and more tolerant outlook than many of his kind. The Warden found himself warming towards his visitor.

"I reckon you do, sir."

"What we offer is an entertainment of a light, but serious tone."

"It's a mite unusual."

"It is simple humanity. We want to bring a touch of relief into your prisoners' hard lives."

"I don't know that I'm employed to make life easier for them," the Warden pointed out. "They're as prime a collection of cut-throats as you could find in the world penned up here. No matter what your intellectual friends tell you, Father, the law doesn't very often make a mistake and send an innocent man to jail."

"I'm not exactly unaware of the existence of sin," the blackclad man said gently.

"Reckon not. But I didn't want you forgetting that you're dealing with criminals."

"Who are also human beings."

"There's some folks who'd give you an argument about that over most of the prisoners in here."

"Don't get me wrong, Warden," Donglar put in hurriedly. "I'm not one of these dreamy-eyed ideologists who invests every thief with a shroud of martyrdom. I know that most men take to crime because they are too damned idle to work, and that nothing will make that kind change for the better. However, there are a few who might be redeemable. You look surprised."

A guilty look flickered on the Warden's face. Having prided himself upon possessing a face which hid his thoughts, he felt surprised at Father Donglar's last words.

"I just never thought to hear you say that, Father."

"Why? Because I came here proposing a small entertainment for the inmates."

"Sure. When I got your first letter, I thought——" The Warden's words trailed off, unsure of how to continue without giving offence.

"You thought, 'Here's another of those fools,'" smiled Donglar. "I do confess there are aspects of prison life I would like to see changed. So would you, Warden. I have heard something of your liberal attitudes."

"I even tried them out; and was sold down the river by the men who I trusted and tried to help. It taught me one thing. Never trust any prisoner."

"You have no trusties here then?"

"Sure, some. But that doesn't mean I'd give them the keys to the main gates, or trust them out of my sight."

"You won't stop my little entertainment though?"

"With that letter you brought from the Governor?" grinned the Warden. "All I do is reserve the right to take precautions."

"Such as?"

"Selecting which prisoners can attend—and posting guards."

"If you believe that to be necessary, go ahead."

"I do, Father."

"Then you'll have no objections from me."

Having come into contact with numerous other "reformers," most of whom appeared to regard the Warden and guards as their enemies, the head of the Penitentiary had not expected such co-operation. Receiving it made him less inclined to object to his visitor's scheme.

"When will you give your sh—entertainment?"

"Tomorrow evening, if we may."

"Feel free. Have you everything you need?"

"Everything but somewhere to seat our audience and make a small stage."

"There's only one place," the Warden declared. "That big building down by the main gates. It holds our wagons, but they can come out for the night."

"May I look it over?" Donglar asked.

"Sure," agreed the Warden, rising. "I'll take you over there right now."

Leaving the office block, the Warden escorted his visitor across an open square to the big wooden building standing at the left of the Gatlin gun-guarded main gates.

"I see you have female prisoners here," Donglar remarked as the Warden unlocked the building's double doors.

Turning, the Warden followed the direction of Donglar's gaze. A woman came from one of the doors in the next building, emptied a bucket into a barrel close by and stood for a moment studying the visitor. She was tall, with blonde hair cut almost boyishly short in accordance with regulations. Good looking, her face held a haughty expression one would not expect to see on a woman in her position. The long white coat she wore was open and showed a full, buxom, yet shapely figure. As prison regulations forbade the wearing of corsets, her waist must slim down naturally, for it curved in under the full bosom and rose out to rounded hips. Even in the rough grey prison dress, she looked a fine figure of womanhood. After the one glance, the woman returned through the door from which she emerged.

"We've a few here," the Warden admitted. "I don't like it, but the Territory can't afford to run a separate penitentiary for women. Not that there's any real need. A woman has to be real bad before any Arizona court'll send her here."

"Will you allow them to see the entertainment?"

"I don't reckon it'd be wise. The men don't see or get near a woman all through their sentence and I wouldn't want to stir them up by putting the female prisoners close to them."

"A wise decision."

Opening the double doors, the Warden stood aside to let his visitor enter the building. Several strongly made prison wagons stood in the large room, the remainder being taken up by sledgehammers, picks, shovels and other tools. At the far end a smaller door offered an alternative exit.

"Perfect," said Father Donglar. "Can we have access through the rear door?"

"I'll have it unlocked."

"Then we'll screen off the far end and the performers can make their entrances through the rear door. We'll have our wagon just outside, that will keep us clear of the main part of the prison."

Once again the Warden found himself admiring his visitor's grasp of the situation and willingness to co-operate. While a humanitarian, the priest was no fool and did not aim to put his party in a position where they might be grabbed by a bunch of desperate prisoners and used as hostages. In view of what he had seen and heard, the Warden reckoned he would do all he could to make the entertainment a success.

"I can't run to fancy curtains, Father," he warned. "But I'll have a couple of the trusties hang some tarps that'll be almost as good—if not as dressy."

"Why, thank you, Warden."

"Just give us a good show tomorrow."

"I think I can safely promise you that."

Soon after, the Warden stood by the main gates and watched his visitor ride off in the direction of the town of Yuma. Studying the way Donglar sat the big, powerful bay horse, the Warden could see that the other knew how to ride. Clearly, Father Donglar was a man of many talents.

Next day, shortly before sundown, the priest returned accompanied by a two-horse wagon driven by a gaunt, elderly man dressed in sober black. At the driver's side sat a tall, shapely, beautiful young woman. Shoulder long black hair hung from under her rather severe hat. While her clothes tried to hide the fact, she showed signs of being very shapely in the large style fashionable at that time. Behind the young woman stood a middle-aged man with a sun-reddened face—in other company, the Warden might have guessed at a different cause for the reddening.

"We have run into a little trouble, Warden," the priest announced as he handed the bay's reins to one of the waiting guards. "Perhaps you can help?"

"Try me and see, Father," the Warden answered.

"It's Miss Garfields' maid. The foolish girl refused to come out here, even though we tried to convince her there was no danger."

"How does that affect me?"

"We've found when doing these entertainments that the effect is better if Miss Garfield appears dressed well. She makes a rather fast change of clothing at one point and needs the assistance of her maid."

"How can I help?" asked the Warden.

"By allowing one of your female prisoners to act as the maid."

"You know what kind of women come in here, Father?" the Warden growled. "Bad Mexicans, Apaches, white trash of the worst kind. I couldn't let a for-real lady like Miss Garfield come into contact with them."

"How about the one I saw yesterday?" asked the priest. "I thought that she looked a woman of breeding."

"Who, Considine?" the Warden answered. "Well, she's not like the other women here, and that's for sure. They're stupid and bad. She's smart, intelligent, well-bred."

"Then why is she in here?"

"She and her mother were working a real smart game up Backsight way. At that time there wasn't much of a town.

The Territorial Land Office put land up for sale on a develop-or-lose-the-deposit contract. Her brother ran the Land Office in Backsight, and she made sure that the folks who paid the deposit never made good on the contract. She killed two men and had a few more killed before she was stopped."

"And who stopped her?"

"That Rio Hondo gun-wizard, Dusty Fog. She was trying to stop the Raines' wagon-train getting through. Captain Fog happened along, took over the train and bust up the game.* Her brother was killed, she took lead herself. Drew a life sentence at her trial. That was almost four years back. She'd've hung, only being a woman saved her."

"What kind of a prisoner is she?" asked the priest.

"Behaves well. I made her a trusty and she helps the doctor. Maybe she'd lend Miss Garfield a hand if we asked her."

"We can but try."

After telling one of the guards to show the driver where to take his wagon, the Warden took Donglar across the exercise yard and into the small building used as a combined surgery and hospital.

"We don't keep Considine with the other women," the Warden explained. "She has a room at the end of the building." He pointed to a door at the end of the passage and the key which hung on a hook alongside it. "Only time the door's locked is at night and the key's always there. Happen there's doctoring work after dark, well, the doc's not always able to handle it, so the guard knocks to wake Considine and lets her out. She's good at doctoring now, the prisoners'd rather have her than the doctor tend to them. When she's finished, she goes back to her room and slams the door. It has a spring lock."

"It seems that one of your prisoners respects your trust, Warden," smiled Donglar.

*Told in *Wagons to Backsight* by J. T. Edson.

"It looks that way," agreed the Warden and knocked on the door. When the woman opened it, he went on, "Father Donglar here needs your help, Considine."

Cold eyes studied the priest as he made his request, then she nodded her head. "Of course I'll help, Warden. I'm tired though, the doctor was—indisposed—last night and I didn't get much sleep through looking after one of the inmates."

"Miss Garfield only needs help to change into the second dress. She'll have time to attend to herself after that," Father Donglar explained.

"You can go straight back to your room after you've helped," the Warden continued. "It's all settled then."

"Come with me, Miss Considine," the priest said and walked towards the wagon at the woman's side, leaving the Warden to go and organize the delivery of the audience.

Although working under primitive conditions, the show passed without any major hitches and was well-received by the men selected to attend. Being unsure of how the prisoners would react, and not wishing to have any trouble arise from allowing his inmates to come into such close contact with people from the outside, the Warden told every available guard to be present. In addition, all but the duty matron of the female staff attended the entertainment, grabbing a chance to make a change from the monotony and risks of their working life.

At last the entertainment ended and the prisoners filed back to the grim, forbidding cell blocks. Joining the priest's party, the Warden thanked them for what had been a much better show than he, secretly, expected.

"Did Considine do all right, Miss Garfield?" he asked.

"She helped me perfectly," the young woman replied. "After she finished, I asked her to see the show, but she said she felt tired and went to that building over there. If you'll excuse me, Warden, I'll change for the trip back to town."

Before he could answer, the girl climbed into the rear of the wagon and dropped the covers. The Warden had planned to search the wagon before it left, knowing the ingenuity prisoners showed in their attempts to escape, but the girl's entrance prevented him giving the order. As no scream or other sound came, he concluded that none of the inmates had in some manner secreted themselves aboard the wagon. So he turned to the priest and started to offer an invitation.

"I hope you'll all be my guests before——"

The words chopped off as a roaring noise rose from one of the cell blocks. Instantly the Warden swung to face the sound, his right hand going under his jacket to where a Merwin and Hulbert Army pocket revolver hung in a shoulder holster.

"Riot!" bellowed a guard's voice.

More shouting, clatters and crashes rose from the other cell blocks as the prisoners caught the infection and added their quota to the tumult. Racing across the exercise yard, a guard halted at the Warden's side.

"Trouble in Twenty-one, Warden!" he reported. "It looks bad!"

"I'll be right over."

At that moment, one of the female compound's matrons came up. "The women've heard it, Warden. They're getting stirred up. We can hold them, but it'll take all of us."

"Try to control it yourselves," the Warden answered, then looked at Father Donglar's party. "I reckon you'd best get your folks out of here, Father. The situation's dangerous, and this'll be no place for a lady."

For an awful, worrying moment the Warden thought that the priest would ask to be taken to the rioters so that he could reason with them. Having seen more than one prison riot, the Warden knew that such attempts seldom brought any results and not infrequently presented the rioters with an opportunity of laying hands upon a useful bargaining piece in the form of a hostage. Then the worry passed as

Father Donglar once more showed his grasp of the facts of life.

"You're right, Warden," he agreed. "Unless I can help——"

"I've got all the help I need," the Warden stated, watching guards armed with ten-gauge twin-barrel shotguns converging on the trouble area.

"Then I'll take my party to safety."

"I'm only sorry this happened tonight," the Warden replied and raised his voice. "Pass out Father Donglar's party, main gate."

"Yo!" boomed back one of the guards, and the double gates swung open.

With barely a glance for his departing guests, the Warden hurried towards the cell block in which the trouble started.

While the matron regarded Considine as a reliable trusty, she knew better than trust any prisoner too far. So, on her way to the female compound, she passed through the hospital block. Taking the key to Considine's cell, she opened the door and peered through the half-light at the shape on the bed. Either Considine slept well, or did not intend becoming involved in any way with the riot; the blanket-covered shape never moved, lying facing the wall, blonde hair all that showed above the covers. Satisfied that all was well, the matron did not enter the room or waste time in speaking. Locking the door again, she pocketed the key and hurried back to the compound.

Although the rioting lasted all night, it proved to be more noisy than dangerous. The warden had seen quieter riots which ended with a number of deaths on both sides. Swift action, grim determination on the part of the guards and no mistaken outside interference by self-professed humanitarians kept the situation in hand. However, it was after sun-up before the prisoners quieted down and the Warden gave the order for normal routine to be resumed.

"Come on, Considine," growled a matron, entering the woman's room. "You're not a lady's maid any mo——"

Stopping speaking, she leapt to the bed and tore off the blanket. Under it lay a dress-maker's dummy, turned on its side and with a white wig in place. Matrons in female prisons were picked more for ability to defend themsleves and handling their charges than for brains; but, smart or not, the one in Considine's cell could add two and two correctly. The cell door had been locked when she arrived and could not be unlocked on the inside, nor did it have a grille through which the prisoner might reach the key. Which meant that Considine had not been in the bed when the matron looked in the previous night. Knowing what must have happened, the matron made for the Warden's office on the run. If Considine had escaped, she must have done so before the matron visited her room. Only once had the gates been open after the riot started—when Father Donglar's party left.

About the time that the matron reached the Warden with news of the escape, three riders allowed their horses to take a blow on top of a rim some thirty miles to the north-east of Yuma.

"The riot should be under control by now," the man in the black clothes remarked, turning in his saddle and looking along their back trail. "They'll most likely have found that you're gone, Anthea."

Dressed now in a Stetson, shirt waist, divided skirt and boots, Anthea Considine winced as she moved in her saddle. Almost four years in prison had been poor training for such a long, hard ride. Catching Miss "Garfield's" slightly mocking gaze, Anthea tried to hide any hint of weakness that might show.

"We've a good start," she told Donglar, and to annoy the other member of the party continued, "You planned everything perfectly, Charles."

Seeing the frown which came to the second girl's face, Donglar replied, "Myra did the planning, Anthea. This little sister of yours is a mighty smart girl. It was she who suggested using the maid idea to get to you and thought of climbing in and starting to change before the Warden could have the wagon searched."

"Charles was wonderful," Myra Considine put in, moving a little closer to the man and eyeing him in a proprietary manner. "He made the contacts in prison, arranged for the riot, fixed up the relay of horses, everything."

"What will be the Warden's actions when he learns of the escape?" Anthea asked, directing her words at the man rather than to her sister.

"He would have telegraphed the surrounding county sheriffs and alerted them," Donglar answered. "But we cut the wires. It'll take time to repair them. Then he'll send word about the wagon, but that won't help any."

One of the services rendered by Donglar to the Considine sisters, although not mentioned by Myra, had been the disposal of the wagon and silencing, with a .41 Remington Double Derringer, the two performers brought along to make up the entertainment. Wagon and corpses now rested in an arroyo bottom, the signs of its leaving the trail having been carefully obliterated and its team turned free. After that, he and the girls took to the waiting horses and began a fast run for freedom.

Knowing that the Warden would expect them to make for Mexico, or over the State line into California, Donglar took them to the north-east. He had relays of good horses spaced along their route, an aid to putting as much distance as possible between them and the Penitentiary before the discovery of Anthea's escape.

"How about my plans for the other matter?" Anthea asked.

"I've taken care of that," Myra replied. "But I can't see why you're going to all that trouble just to take your revenge."

"Can't you?" her sister spat out.

"Because of your brother?" Donglar suggested.

"Partly. But mainly because of the past four years. I've been cooped up in that stinking hell-hole, cut off from everything that makes life worthwhile. All that time only one thing kept me from suicide. The thought of getting my revenge on

those who put me there. Now I'm free, I intend to have it. I'm
going to make that rebel scum in Backsight wish they'd never
left their Virginia homes — and I'm going to see Dusty Fog
dead."

CHAPTER TWO

The Name Is Dusty Fog

Over the years, the bartender at the Cool Beer Saloon in Junction City had become a keen student of human nature and formed the habit of practicing his hobby on such newcomers as chanced to visit the small town on the Arizona-New Mexico border. Two subjects worthy of his attention stood at his bar shortly after sundown one evening.

Texans, or the bartender missed his guess. One could not mistake the shape and style of those low-crowned, wide-brimmed genuine J. B. Stetson hats. Even without having seen it, the bartender guessed any decorations on their boots would include the traditional Texan star motif.

One of the pair stood around the six-foot mark and, though young, showed a powerful build. Not yet nineteen years of age, the subject carried himself with a certain assurance and quiet competence. His black hat sat on blond hair, shoved back so no shadow fell on a tanned, healthy, strong, handsome face with clear blue eyes. A tight-rolled bandana trailed, long ends down, over his shirt. The brown levis pants hung cowhand style outside his boots. Around his waist was strapped a well-made gunbelt with a brace of staghorn handled Colt Artillery Peacemakers reposing in a significant manner in the holsters. A fine figure of self-reliant manhood, the bartender mused, yet completely over-shadowed by his companion.

Come to a real fine point, the bartender conceded that the second of his subjects was just about as fine a physical specimen as he had ever seen.

A good three inches taller than his companion, the second man had a great spread of shoulders and tapered down to a lean waist and long, straight, powerful legs. The white Stetson on his curly, golden blond hair sported a silver concha-decorated band. His face, while almost classically handsome, showed intelligence and strength. Unless the bartender guessed wrong, the bandana was real silk. That shirt had been made of finest material to its wearer's measure as had his levis; such a giant frame could not be fitted off the shelves of a store. The finely-tooled gunbelt told a tale to Western eyes, in the way it carried two ivory-butted Colt Cavalry Peacemakers just right for *real* fast withdrawal and use.

Handsome, something of a dandy—but all man, was the bartender's summing up of the blond giant. Maybe a rich rancher, or the son of one; yet his hands showed the signs of hard work.

It being a slack time, the bartender tried to decide on the relationship between the two blonds. Although the taller man treated his companion with almost brotherly tolerance, addressing him as "Boy" and being called Mark in return, they showed no family resemblance. While the youngster dressed well, his clothing did not come up to the giant's in value. Maybe they were employer and employee; in the West such tended to mingle on a more friendly basis than in the staid East. Before the bartender could devise a way to satisfy his curiosity, an interruption came which took his mind off the matter.

The batwing doors thrust open and a tall young man entered. Blond, handsome, well-built and dressed to the height of Texas range fashion, the newcomer wore a brace of white-handled guns butt forward for a cross-hand draw. However his words rather than his appearance attracted the attention of the saloon's patrons.

"The name is Dusty Fog," he announced. "Belly up to the bar, boys. I'm setting them up."

While preparing for the rush to answer the request, the bartender gave the new arrival a long scrutiny and felt just a little mite disappointed. It had been just the same when he first saw Wyatt Earp and found, instead of a god-like figure of a man, a person, who looked like a prosperous trail-end town undertaker. Sure the newcomer looked good, yet he did not come quite up to how one expected a man with such a reputation to be. At seventeen Dusty Fog commanded Company "C" of the Texas Light Cavalry and built a reputation as being one of the Confederate States Army's top fighting cavalry leaders. Twice since the end of the war he had been sent into Mexico to handle missions of the greatest national importance.* Since leaving the disbanded C.S.A., Dusty Fog had become known as a top-grade cowhand, segundo of the biggest ranch in Texas, trail boss of the first water, town-taming lawman. Men called him the Rio Hondo gun-wizard and claimed him to be the fastest, most accurate of the masters of the pistol arts.

From his appearance, the newcomer fitted Dusty Fog's age, but the bartender expected something more of a man with such varied claims to fame.

Glancing at the first two objects of his interest, the bartender saw "Boy" throw an angry look of such concentrated force towards the newcomer that it came almost as a shock. Even as eager customers swarmed forward, "Boy" started to move in the newcomer's direction. Reaching out with a big hand, Mark caught "Boy's" arm and held him. After saying something that the bartender did not catch, Mark walked out of the room followed by his companion; the

*Told in *The Ysabel Kid* and *The Peacemakers*.

latter throwing more angry glares at the man called Dusty Fog.

Among the customers who accepted the newcomer's offer were three unshaven, hard-faced men who entered shortly after dark, took a table near the door and positioned themselves so that each could watch the other's backs. Returning to their seats, they studied their temporary host with interest.

"Reckon it is, Dave?" asked the middle-sized member of the trio, running fingers through dark red hair.

"Could be," answered the tallest. "Did you ever see Fog afore, Walt?"

"Naw," answered the last man. "I was fixing to go to Mulrooney from Brownton, but changed my mind when I heard how he handled the first train-load who tried to move in."†

"He's a mite smaller'n I expected, all I've heard about him," Dave said doubtfully. "Why not go over and ask him, Rusty."

"Oh sure," the red head snorted. "I can see me going over there and saying, 'Are you the for-real Dusty Fog?'"

"We'd not be kept waiting long for an answer," grinned Walt. "Trouble being that you wouldn't be there to hear it."

For a time the trio sat watching the newcomer buying drinks for a selection of bar-flies and boasting of his exploits as marshal of Quiet Town and Mulrooney.

"He's got enough money," Dave commented. "That figures, Ole Devil Hardin's his uncle and about the richest man in Texas."

"I could sure use some of that five thousand dollars," Walt remarked wistfully. "Only I don't fancy——"

Dave gave a gesture which chopped off whatever sage comments Walt might be prepared to share. In the silence following the signal, the newcomer's voice reached them.

"Drink up, boys. I'm just going out back, and when I

†Told in *The Trouble Busters*.

come in I'll tell you about how I won those gold-mounted Colts at the Cochise Country Fair."*

Thrusting back his chair, Dave rose and walked out of the front door, an example closely followed by his companions. Glancing back, they saw the newcomer walking regally across the room with pauses to speak to various customers. Dave led the way to the end of the building.

Being situated in what regarded itself as a progressive town, the owner of the saloon attempted to illuminate all the side alley which led to his back-house. Although he hung lamps in strategic positions, only the one outside the side door remained; that one could be seen shining through the transom window, making stealing it too risky for the local poor Mexican population to chance. However the light given by the remaining lamp would be sufficient for their purposes. In addition to illuminating the user of the door, it would put him in a position where he had to look from light into darkness.

"No guns, you *loco bobos!*" Dave warned, seeing his companions reach hipward as the door opened. "I'll handle it with this."

And with those words, he drew the long-bladed Green River knife from its sheath at his belt. Knowing his ability in the matter of throwing a knife, the others raised no objections. Yet as they saw the tall young man emerge from the saloon, both felt doubts creep in. Raising his right hand, Dave gauged the distance with his eye and felt tension bite at him. He realised, as did the other two, that if the knife missed, or failed to produce sufficient agony on its arrival, at least one of them stood a better than even chance of dying before their victim's guns.

"Throw it!" hissed Walt, hand on the butt of his gun.

Soft though they had been, the words carried to the young man's ears, and he started to turn. Realisation of what that

*Told in *Gun Wizard.*

meant spurred Dave into action. Around lashed his arm and the knife flew forward. It went a mite low, aimed at striking the victim's kidney region from behind. In turning, the victim spoiled Dave's plan; but the result proved to be almost as effective. A look of shock came to the young man's face, yet he did not react with the devilish speed one might have expected from stories told about him. Instead he froze for the vital instant necessary for the knife to reach him. Dave could claim to be something of an expert with a knife and certainly made good his frequent boasts that night. The spear point of the knife took his victim just under the breast bone, sinking into his solar plexus. While not quite as effective as striking the kidney region, it proved sufficient for their needs. Air burst from the stricken man's lungs as agony jack-knifed him over. Clutching at the hilt of the knife, he sank to his knees.

"Get the gunbelt!" Dave yelled and dashed forward with his companions on his heels.

Reaching the injured man, Rusty bent down and shoved him to the ground. Ignoring the blood which followed in a spurt when Dave jerked free the knife, Rusty began to un-buckle their victim's gunbelt. Walt muttered something in a low voice and suddenly realised the vulnerability of their position. With that thought in mind, he turned to look back the way they came—and received the shock of his life.

So intent had the trio been on watching for their victim, then filled with nervous tension when he appeared that they gave no thought to their danger. None took the precautions they might have done when preparing to attack and rob a normal man. In failing to follow the rules of their illegal profession, they made a fatal mistake. Not one of the trio had thought to look up and down the street before ap-proaching the business in hand. If they had done so, things might have worked out differently for them.

Sitting a low-horned, double-girthed saddle on a huge blood-bay stud horse, the cowhand called Mark rode with his companion from one of the stores further along the street. "Boy" used the same type of rig—naturally as it was standard Texas range equipment—straddling a big, powerful paint stallion and leading a loaded pack horse. Clearly, something still annoyed the youngster for he threw an angry gesture towards the saloon.

"Damn it to hell, Mark," he protested. "Can't I just go in——"

"No," Mark interrupted with a grin. "Happen we take any longer in getting back with these supplies, Du—Down there!"

Following the direction of Mark's eyes, "Boy" saw the three hard-cases gathered around their victim. Rusty's blood-smeared hands had completed the unbuckling of the gunbelt and Dave gripped the victim's shirt ready to raise the body.

Swiftly the blond giant swung from his saddle and headed towards the alley on the run. Dropping from the paint and leaving it standing with trailing reins, "Boy" followed. Not on his friend's heels, but swinging clear of him in a manner which allowed unrestricted use of the staghorn handled Colts should it become necessary. In view of what they found the trio doing, and considering the very sensible attitude Western folks took to robbery and murder, most likely the guns would be needed.

Walt saw the approach of the two men, yelled a warning to his companions and grabbed at the butt of his gun. Without breaking his stride, the blond giant replied to Walt's threatening gesture. Mark's hand made a flashing move, three of the fingers curling around the butt of the right-side Colt, thumb hooking over its hammer and starting to draw back, forefinger entering the trigger-guard as the barrel cleared leather and slanted away from him; all in the smooth, effortless-looking, yet incredibly fast manner which marked the difference between a true master of the art and an average performer. Just three-quarters of a second after Mark's first move, Walt took lead. Not a bad time considering the Cavalry model of the Peacemaker carried a seven and a half inch barrel, giving it an overall length of twelve and a half inches and weighing two pounds, five ounces. Caught in the chest by a .45 bullet, his own gun barely clear of leather, Walt spun around and crashed to the ground.

Hearing Walt's warning yell, Dave released his hold of the moaning, badly-wounded man and swung around to meet the threat to his freedom and life. Although Dave proved to be faster than Walt, he still lacked the necessary extra edge of speed so necessary to stay alive at such a time. "Boy's" right hand made a move almost identical to his companion's in speed and execution. Only an instant after the blond giant cut down Walt, flame lashed from the five-and-a-half-inch Artillery barrel of "Boy's" offside Colt. He threw lead just as accurately as had Mark, sending two hundred and fifty grains of conical-shaped lead into Dave's head. In a way Dave achieved more than had Walt, for he got off one shot in reply; his bullet passing through the wall of the adjacent building, a store, and was subsequently found to have pierced a new keg of molasses.

Still crouched over the victim and clutching the gunbelt in his hands, Rusty saw his friends struck down. Loyalty decreed that he take up their cause and try to extract vengeance for their deaths. Common sense told him that the two Texans belonged in a far higher class of the gun fighting arts than to which he could aspire. Besides, Dave and Walt were not good friends. Came to a fact, on might call them no more than business associates, not successful associates at that; barely more than casual acquaintances. Rusty concluded that the decrees of loyalty did not apply in that case.

With his conscience salved—in a remarkably short space of time—Rusty used his crouching position in much the same manner as a runner in a sprint race when the starting gun sounded. Still holding the gunbelt, he hurled himself away from the victim and hit full speed in two strides as he tore towards the welcome safety of darkness beyond the lamp's light.

"Halt!" roared a voice from the street. "Halt or I'll stop you."

Having a better than fair idea of his fate if he obeyed, Rusty decided to chance taking a bullet and kept moving. He heard the flat, angry "Splat!" of a close passing bullet merge with the crack of a shot as a bullet hissed by his head. Dropping the gunbelt as an unneeded encumbrance, he almost threw himself around the corner of the saloon and out of sight.

"Want for me to take out after him, Mark?" asked "Boy" as they walked along the alley.

"Leave him to the local law," Mark replied.

Had the bartender been present, he might have read much significance in the way the Texans comported themselves. Even while speaking, neither took his eyes for a moment from the man he had shot, and each carried his Colt cocked ready for use. Judging by their actions, they might have been trained and efficient peace officers handling a routine piece of range-country business.

After the shooting there had been considerable shouting inside the saloon, but nobody committed the folly of throwing open the side door. Feet pounded and the front entrance burst open as men came out and made their way towards the alley. Attracted by the shooting, the town marshal—a leathery old-timer with long experience behind a badge— loped up carrying the most useful argument in a crisis, a twin-barrelled, ten-gauge shotgun.

"What happened?" he asked, thrusting through the crowd and looking to where Mark knelt by the victim and "Boy" stood beyond him so as to watch for the unlikely event of the fleeing man making his return.

"Those two and another jumped him for some reason," Mark explained, indicating the two shot men and their victim. "Get a doctor here *pronto*. He's still alive but bleeding like a stuck pig."

"He's Dusty Fog, Marshal!" yelled one of the crowd. "That's why they laid for him."

"Dusty Fog, huh?" replied the marshal, sounding just a mite impressed.

"Told us so hisself," confirmed the informant.

"And he lied in his teeth," "Boy" stated, turning and walking back to the waiting marshal.

"You reckon so, young feller?"

"I *know* so, Marshal."

So saying, the youngster twirled his Colt on a trained forefinger and offered it butt first to the peace officer. While no longer in his prime, the marshal possessed a keen pair of eyes which detected certain marks upon the deep blue of the Colt's Best Citizen's Finish metal. Accepting the gun, he read the words engraved on its backstrap.

"To our pard, Waco, from Ole Devil's Floating Outfit."

"Waco, huh," he said and his gaze turned to the blond giant. "You'll be Mark Counter, I reckon."

Listening to the names, the bartender felt like kicking himself for his lack of foresight. Taking all things into consideration, he ought to have guessed the big blond's identity. Of course when the wounded man entered and called himself Dusty Fog, the connection ought to have leapt instantly to mind. In exculpation the bartender could claim to have been fully occupied serving customers at the time when his brain should have made the deduction. The reason for the younger Texan's annoyance and need for his being prevented from remonstrating with the false claimant now stood crystal clear and explained. Both he and Mark had good reason to know the newcomer lied on the matter of his identity.

Since their first meeting in Mexico just after the Civil War ended, Mark Counter had become known as Dusty Fog's right bower and all-but inseparable companion; one of the reasons why the bartender did not connect the names was that the two men and one other could almost always be found together.

However the bartender could take comfort in the knowledge that many of his observations on Mark's character proved correct. The son of a rich rancher and wealthy in his own right since a maiden aunt left him all her considerable fortune, Mark could also claim to be a cowhand second to none and a master of his trade. Many tales made the rounds on the subject of his giant strength and skill in a roughhouse brawl. Living in the shadow of the Rio Hondo gun-wizard, Mark's ability as a skilled gun-fighter tended to be overlooked, but many competent judges placed him a close second to Dusty Fog in the matter of speedy withdrawal and accurate use of a brace of Colts.

During the previous three years Waco's name had risen to considerable prominence in connection with the exploits of the elite of the O.D. Connected ranch's crew, Ole Devil Hardin's floating outfit. While he bore only the one name, that did not prevent him from gaining the reputation for being a good man to have around in time of trouble. Left an orphan almost from birth, by a Waco Indian raid on a wagon train, he had been raised by one of the travelling families. At thirteen he left his foster home to look for a new life. Even in those early days he owned, wore and could use a gun; an old Navy Colt which took one man's life. By seventeen he rode for Clay Allison's wild onion crew and stood at the head of the slippery slope down which more than one handy Texas boy slid into the life of a wanted man on the run. Then he met up dramatically with the Rio Hondo gun-wizard—in fact Dusty Fog pulled Waco almost from under the hooves of a stampeding herd of cattle*— and from then began a steady change. From a proddy, suspicious trigger-fast-and-up-from-Texas kid, he changed into a friendly and useful member of rangeland society. While regarding and treating him as a favourite young brother, the other members of the floating outfit taught him all they could and gave him a practical education of some breadth

*Told in *Trigger Fast*.

in its scope. They called him "Boy," a name he would take only from a select few, but implied in saying the word that he would soon grow up into a real good man.

"How about them two?" asked the marshal, nodding to where men bent examining the two shot hard-cases.

"This'n's done," said the man by Dave.

"I reckon this jasper'll live to stretch hemp," continued another.

"Wonder why they jumped that young feller?" the marshal said, watching the local doctor bend over the victim.

"He was toting a fair wad of money," the bartender answered.

"Only they looked to be more concerned with taking his gunbelt than searching his pockets," Waco put in.

"A good gunbelt and brace of Colt's worth something," the marshal pointed out.

"Sure, maybe fifty or so dollars. Inside there, he flashed four times that much in cash money and wouldn't have spent more than twenty or thirty bucks."

Studying Waco's face, the marshal nodded. "Makes a change to see a young feller as uses his head for more'n a hatrack. Could be these fellers believed he was Dusty Fog and aimed to make a reputation by shooting him."

"Except that he's been hit by a knife," Mark commented dryly.

"Feller gets to my age, he don't see things as quick as you young'uns," the marshal answered. "Reckon Cap'n Fog's made a few enemies in his time. Could be one of them three was one."

"Well, I can't lay claim to knowing all Dusty's enemies," Mark replied, "but that bunch don't put me in mind of anybody we tangled with."

"Could've been hired for it," Waco suggested. "Took the gunbelt to prove they'd earned their pay."

"And just happened to be in here?" grunted Mark.

"Why not? We haven't made any secret about taking

those blood horses to Colonel Raines's place and Junction City's the most likely place for us to come to happen we need supplies."

"He'll live," the doctor commented, rising from the victim. "I'll have him moved down to my place when I've looked at this other jasper."

"See if that pair's got anything in their pockets that might tell us where they come from or what they're doing here," the marshal ordered and looked at Mark. "Happen they'd been hired, they'd likely know the man they wanted. Don't reckon that feller's so all-fired like Cap'n Fog that they'd make a mistake."

"Not if they knew Dusty at all," agreed Mark.

Thinking of the Rio Hondo gun-wizard's reputation, and studying the victim, the marshal could hardly believe the attackers made a mistake after being hired to kill Dusty Fog. Why that young feller there wouldn't have the heft of Mark Counter, and the marshal reckoned Dusty Fog must be an even bigger man than the blond giant.

"There's this sheet of paper in his pocket," said the man searching Dave's body, preventing the marshal from commenting on his thoughts.

Taking the folded paper, the marshal opened it and looked down. For once his face showed emotion. Surprise and disbelief crept across his leathery features and he held the paper towards Mark.

"Take a look at this," the peace officer said.

"Hell-fire!" Mark ejaculated a moment later. "This's impossible."

"It sure as hell is!" agreed Waco, grabbing the paper and reading its message. "What'll we do. It tells us why they were after Dusty."

"If you don't need us any more, Marshal," Mark said, ignoring the youngster's question. "We'll take it with us and ride. The sooner I can show it to Dusty, the happier I'll feel."

CHAPTER THREE

Wanted Dead, $5,000 Reward

To Eastern eyes, the majority of Western men dressed in much the same manner no matter what their trade or vocation. Almost every man wore a wide brimmed hat, an open-necked shirt, a bandana handkerchief of alarming size around the throat, trousers of levis or denim design, boots, and sported a weapon belt carrying one or two holstered revolvers if nothing more. There were, of course, exceptions. Townsmen tended to follow Eastern city fashions; how close they came to the current trend depended on the proximity of stagecoach or rail services which gave access to more cultural areas and the size of their home town. Professional gamblers, bartenders, preachers of the various religious sects all inclined towards a traditional style. Army scouts still could be found in a few areas wearing fringed buckskin after the fashion of the long-departed mountain men. For the rest of the West's population, the Easterner could rarely differentiate between cowhand, miner, freighter, nester or any of the range country's less publicised trades.

No Western man experienced such difficulty. While the Stetson hat, or one of its copies, might be standard head wear, a man's home State could be told from the shape and manner of wearing. Only a Texan born and raised ever achieved the correct, "jack-deuce" angle over the off eye which marked the son of the Lone Star State.

Bandanas also possessed universal appeal; and not merely as a piece of ornamental decoration or open-necked shirt's tie. Knotted and hung on the most handy peg available, the neck, it served a number of purposes, from nostril cleaner and protector to sling in case of emergency, and was easily reached without the necessity of fumbling in the pants pocket.

Shirts told a little. While a miner often rolled up his sleeves, the cowhand rarely did so. Most of the cowhand's work was done on the back of a horse and chasing cattle through bushes proved less painful with the shirt's sleeves down to cover the arms.

Pants offered a much better idea of a man's employment. A sod-busting nester might wear bib overalls, but no cowhand or miner would. The miner, wishing to keep flying stone chips and dirt out of his boots, tucked his trouser cuffs into them. Leaving his outside the boots, a cowhand turned back the cuffs to act as a repository for nails when performing a task requiring them.

Of all, boots offered the plainest indication. The cowhand sported high heels with which to spoke the ground and hold firm when roping afoot, or grip better in the rain-slicked stirrups of a running horse. Miners and sod-busters, being of a less equestrian turn, preferred low heels and heavier footwear.

A student of Western men might have written a treatise on the subject of saddles as a means of establishing identity and home. Men of Wyoming and the adjacent areas preferred the Cheyenne roll rig designed by Frank Meanea in 1870 and which offered a long leather flange over the rear of the cantle board as an aid to stability. In California the range rider went into action afork a saddle with a soup-plate sized horn, single girth and round saddle skirts. Down in Texas, a square-skirted, low horned, doubled girthed rig was *de rigueur*. The Texan tied his rope to the saddle when throwing it—figuring to hang on to whatever he caught—instead of dallying the end ready for quick release in an emergency, which was the habit of lesser men.

So it may be seen that, to Western eyes, no two types of employment wore identical clothing.

While the eight riders approaching the halted group of wagons might dress and look like cowhands, at least one person present and watching them read the signs correctly.

Seated on a packing trunk at the side of one of the seven wagons, an obviously Texas-raised cowhand threw a searching glance in the direction of the distant riders and then gave his attention to the man at his side. No Texan, this second traveller. He wore a Stetson, but not in the fashion of a range-bred citizen. Although he had discarded his coat, the collarless shirt, trousers and town shoes marked him as a dude. Tall, in his middle twenties, pleasant featured, he showed all the unmistakable signs of one expecting the momentary arrival of his first child.

"It's awful quiet in there," he said, for the seventh time in ten minutes and threw a nervous glance towards the wagon.

"Well now, I'll tell you one thing," replied the cowhand in his lazy Texas drawl. "I've never yet known Doc to blow one out with dynamite."

For a moment Maurice Caldwell glared down at the cowhand, then a faint smile wiped away his annoyance at the other's levity and indifference over so important and earth-shattering an event as took place in the Caldwell wagon. Caldwell could safely say that the event would never have come to other than tragedy had the cowhand's party not arrived.

The wagons, taking a party of assorted migrants to the fast-growing town of Backsight, carried a number of women qualified to attend a normal birth. Unfortunately Caldwell's wife ran into the kind of difficulties only a doctor could handle. Even as the train's scout prepared to make the long dash to Junction City, knowing he had no chance of getting there and back with a doctor in time, the Texan and two companions came on the scene driving a herd of excellently-bred horses. Although only stopping on the chance of obtaining a meal, the men heard of the trouble and acted immediately. Strangely as it at first seemed, the cowhand seated at Caldwell's side gave the orders. Telling one of his companions to move the remuda out a piece and hold it, he informed the travellers that the third Texan would take a look into the situation. Caldwell's feeble objections— he had reached the point where he was willing to snatch at any straws—were swept aside in a spate of medical terms applied correctly and mingled with profanity from the one designated to do the looking. From that point, smoothly and without shouting or bombast, the leader of the trio took complete control. Selecting one of the women to assist his companion, he chivvied the rest about their duties. A couple of boys went out to help the second Texan hold the grazing horse herd and the rest of the travellers continued following the routine established during the trip west from the distant railhead.

Why had it appeared so strange that such an obviously capable man acted as leader of the trio?

The answer was simple; he did not look the part—at first. In height he stood a mere five foot six, and each of his companions could top that by at least six inches. Not that he appeared puny. In fact the spread to his shoulders and general muscular development hinted at strength far beyond his small size. While he wore expensive clothing, he contrived to make them look like somebody's cast-offs. From black Stetson hat to fancy-stitched boots, he could not be mistaken for other than a Texas cowhand and Western eyes would place him as one of the first water. Small, insignificant he might appear, but when he looked at a man and gave his low-spoken orders, the one listening forgot his lack of inches, feeling latent power and personal magnetism of the dusty blond-haired cowhand. While he wore a finely-constructed gunbelt with matched bone handled Colt Civilian Peacemakers butt forward in the holsters, he did not try to show them off in an attempt to increase his stature.

Hearing the sound of the approaching horses, Caldwell turned and studied the newcomers.

"Strangers," he said. "Cowhands, I'd say."

While knowing that Caldwell said wrong, the small Texan did not correct him. True the new arrivals wore range clothing of general cowhand style, but to Western eyes they were following a far more sinister profession. Maybe sometimes they hired on a cattle spread, only it would be their guns which did the work and not branding iron or rope. Hired fighting men, taking pay for throwing lead, loyal only as long as the money flowed. The small Texan studied and did not like what he saw. One only saw turkey vultures gather in numbers around a kill. So it was with hired guns; seeing eight in a bunch had a certain significance to Western eyes.

A frown came to the small cowhands' face as he watched the men continue to advance right into the rough circle of wagons. All around the camp, people stopped their activities to gaze at the newcomers. The small Texan alone knew that a breach of rangeland etiquette had been committed. In polite circles one waited for an invitation to ride into a strange camp and stayed in the middle until asked to get down and take something.

"Hey you, dude," growled the bearded hard-case who appeared to be the leader of the party. "You got food and coffee going?"

"Some," Caldwell admitted, not caring for the visitor's attitude but remembering all he had heard and seen of range country hospitality.

"Tell the women-folk to get it," ordered the bearded man and swung down from his horse. "Just look around, boys. We want grub, fresh hosses and some blankets. Anything else you need, these folks'll be tickled all ways to give you."

"Suppose you put weight on that saddle and get the hell out of here?" said the small Texan, rising to his feet.

For a moment the bearded hard-case's face held a broad grin as he looked at the small cowhand. Then in some mysterious manner the small figure stood small no more but seemed to have put on height until he dominated the scene. The bearded man rapidly changed his original thought that he faced a chance-drifter who hoped to impress the pretty little gals on the train with his courage.

"We're eight to one, *hombre*," he warned.

"I can count," the Texan answered. "Likewise know there's a *real* accurate rifle lined on you from out there a piece."

A bluff?

If so, it was one of top grade. Not by so much as a flicker of an eye-lid did the Texan show any sign that he might be lying. .

The eight men worked at a dangerous profession, and in it one learned to recognise the real thing real early—or retired permanently and quickly. Small the challenger might be, but he gave seconds to no man in the matter of gun handling. Not one of them possessed the necessary speed to stand alone in a shooting match against the Texan and be alive at the end of it. Collectively they could take him; but two, and maybe more, would die before they dropped him.

Almost thirty seconds ticked by while the matter fermented. While seven of the party waited for the eighth to give them a lead, he knew that *he* would be the Texan's first mark should he make a wrong move.

From the Caldwell wagon came the sound of a slap, followed by the wail of a new-born baby. Instantly, Caldwell headed towards the wagon—and committed the incredible blunder of coming between his protector and the eight men. It was a chance far too good to miss.

.

"Take him!" roared the bearded man, hand stabbing down to his gun.

Being more used to such situations than was Caldwell, the small Texan knew the danger and acted on it. He threw himself clear of the dude's impeding body, going down in a dive and with his hands crossing in an incredibly fast movement. Even as he landed on the ground, his left hand Colt roared. The bearded man's gun was out, swinging in the small Texan's direction, when a .45 bullet drove up under his chin and burst out through the top of his head.

So sudden had been the act that not one of the mounted men managed to make a move before their leader died. One of the flank riders of the party let his hand drop and brought clear his gun. From outside the circle came the flat crack of a rifle, and the man let out a screech as a bullet ripped through his arm. Shock sent him tumbling from his horse, the gun dropping out of useless fingers.

Caldwell had just reached his wagon when he was almost knocked flying by a shape which erupted from inside. Tall, slim, with a studious face that resisted all efforts of the elements to tan it, the man who bounded from the wagon wore cowhand clothes and carried an ivory handled Colt Civilian Model Peacemaker in his blood-smeared right hand. From the casually efficient manner in which he held the gun, it was obvious that he stood high in the *pistolero* line.

Already the unseen rifleman reduced the odds which originally favoured the hard-cases. The arrival of the slim man took the odds down to a point where none of the remaining six intended to play the game.

"I'm getting out of it!" yelled one of their number.

Nothing worked faster than panic. Whirling their horses and ignoring their wounded companion, the six men put spurs to work and raced away from the wagons. So quickly had it happened that none of the train's travellers knew for sure what came off. The wounded man yelled after his departing companions, screaming curses at the desertion. Seeing the two Texans approaching him, the imprecations died off. There was something familiar about the manner in which the two young men moved. For a moment the wounded man could not place what it was. Then the light came. They advanced in the cautious manner of a pair of trained lawmen closing in to take a prisoner who foolishly resisted arrest. The thought led to others. Considering the speed with which the small Texan moved, and adding the knowledge to certain other itmes such as how he wore his guns, the hard-case felt he could say a name. Thinking of that name sent a chill through the wounded man.

Kicking aside the wounded hard-case's revolver, the slim man bent down and studied the injury.

"Through the bicep. Reckon old Lon's losing his sighting eye, or getting religion, Dusty?"

"One or the other," replied the small man. "Best patch him up. Say, what'd you get in there?"

"A boy. I'd say seven and a half pound, but the pappy'll swear it's nearer to ten."

"You—you're Doc Leroy of the Wedge," the wounded man suddenly stated.

"You've been peeking," growled the slim cowhand. "I'll tend to your arm as soon as I've washed off the blood. Happen you feel like dying afore I get back—go right ahead."

Recalling an item of news he had heard in connection with Doc Leroy, the hard-case felt even more certain he could say who fate threw him in contact with. In the recently-ended days of the greater inter-State trail drives from Texas to the Kansas rail-heads, Doc Leroy rode for the Wedge; an outfit of contract herders which took cattle north for small ranchers who could not afford to run their limited numbers of stock to the railroad. Every man of the Wedge could claim to be a tophand at the specialised business of trailing cattle and Doc Leroy's name stood high on their honor list. He gained his name due to having spent two years in an Eastern medical school before circumstances drove him back to Texas and into the life of a trail-driving cowhand. Not that he discarded the learning but continued to study by reading books and working with doctors in the towns he visited. On the trail Doc mended broken bones, diagnosed and treated illnesses, occasionally—as today— delivered babies, and knew more than most top-grade Eastern surgeons ever learned about the removal of bullets from the human body. Rumor held that he had attained considerable ability at putting bullets in when needed also. Earlier that year a notorious hired killer fell before Doc Leroy's gun, dying of a case of slow and in a fair fight.*

Recently Doc had changed employment, the wounded man recalled. With the end of the great drives, Stone Hart gave up trail-bossing herds and took his own ranch. While on his way to join his old boss, Doc fell in with Waco and accepted an offer to become a member of the O.D. Connected where he rode with the floating outfit.

In which case, all things considered, the small man must be the Rio Hondo gun-wizard, Dusty Fog.

As if to give confirmation to the theory, a tall figure carrying a magnificent Winchester Model 1873 rifle strode into the camp. Every item of his clothing was black, even the gunbelt which supported a walnut handled Colt Dragoon butt forward at the right side and a sheathed James Black bowie knife on the left. He had raven black hair and a babyishly innocent-looking handsome face tanned to almost Indian-darkness. Red hazel eyes as wild and savage as a cougar's studied the wounded man, sending shivers up and down his spine.

Even without being able to read the engraving on the inlaid silver plate in the black walnut butt of the rifle, the hard-case knew himself to be in the presence of Loncey Dalton Ysabel—better known as the Ysabel Kid. The knowledge gave him no great joy or comfort.

*Told in *The Hard Riders*.

Born of a French-Creole-Comanche mother and Irish-Kentuckian father, raised and schooled in Mexico and by his maternal grandfather's Dog Soldier lodge brothers, the Kid grew into a deadly dangerous fighting man. The French-Creole had always been knife-handlers of note and he did not shame them when using that deadly product of James Black's Arkansas forge. Nor did he fall below the standards of the Comanche in the matter of horse-mastership. Kentucky bred riflemen of note and the Kid could hold his own with the best of the straight-shooting hill folk of the Blue-grass State. Less of a cowhand than any of his friends in the floating outfit, the Kid acted as scout and look-out. He could read sign if any lay visible to human eyes, move in silence through the thickest bush and live off the country in the manner of his lodge brothers in the greatest, most savage of all the Comanche war clans. Not a man to be troubled by scruples when dealing with an enemy, the Ysabel Kid filled the wounded hard-case with forebodings.

Several of the boys belonging to the train started to move forward, half-scared, half-eager to see what a dead man looked like. Dusty turned from the wounded man and growled at the youngsters to keep back. Then he gave his attention to disposing of the body. Neither dead nor wounded hard-case's horse had gone far, being trained in the range fashion to stand still when the reins trailed free before it. Each man's saddle carried a bulky bedroll, telling of a warbag stowed inside the tarpaulin-covered blankets and suggans.

"How about the remuda, Lon?" he asked.

"I left 'em down in the bottomland by the river," the Kid replied. "They're on good feed and not likely to go far. Those couple of kids I took out with me can hold them in all right."

"Then get that *hombre's* bedroll, use a blanket to cover him. Two of these gents here'll lend a hand with the burying."

"Wish I'd said the hosses were scattered now," the Kid groaned. His eyes went to the wounded man, studying the bleeding arm nursed by the other. "Damned if my barrel's not leaded; I never figured to miss by that much."

"Likely," said Dusty dryly. "Get moving, you danged Comanche."

"I'm going, I'm going. Come on, you two gents."

Looking a mite green around the gills, two of the train's men joined the Kid. The way Dusty saw it, the men would maybe need to know about handling a dead body before they reached their destination, and the sooner they learned, the better. Guessing what Dusty had in mind, the Kid detailed one man to fetch a couple of shovels and asked the other to collect a blanket from the corpse's bedroll.

"Bet I know who'll do the digging," Doc commented, coming from where he had washed the blood off his hands.

"An old Comanche witch-woman once told me I was too delicate to ride the blister end of a shovel," the Kid replied. "Which same I believe her."

"He's got an answer for everything," Dusty remarked.

"Red brother needs one when he's dealing with tricky pale-faces," grunted the Kid and went to supervise the unloading of the bedroll.

Pain and loss of blood had caused the hard-case to lapse into unconsciousness and Doc dropped to one knee ready to begin work. To one side the Kid caught the dead man's horse and started to unstrap the bedroll. Dusty watched his friends at work and then turned his gaze around the camp. All the women had disappeared into the wagons and taken the children with them, which put one worry out of his way. Swiftly his mind turned over the details of the shooting, and he felt perturbed at certain aspects of the affair which he knew to be wrong.

While unrolling the bundle taken from the horse, the Kid saw a familiar-looking sheet of paper sticking among the blankets. He reached for, took up and unfolded the paper, finding much what he expected in the opening words.

"WANTED DEAD
$5,000 REWARD."

It might have been the normal poster put out by a law enforcement office that the Kid held, until he read the name of the wanted man—it was Dusty Fog.

CHAPTER FOUR

Make Talk With Pasear Hennessey

"Just take a look at this," the Kid said, holding out the poster for his friends to see.

"Is it a joke, Dusty?" asked Doc.

"If it is," the Rio Hondo gun-wizard replied quietly, "I'm not laughing."

"For five thousand dollars, every bounty hunter and two-bit gun-slick west of the Pecos'll be after your hide," the Kid growled. "There'll be more than one fixing to kill you, Dusty."

"What do you aim to do about it?" Doc inquired.

"Stop them," answered Dusty Fog.

At that moment Caldwell left his wagon and approached the Texans, meaning to thank Doc. His eyes went to the reward poster, then lifted to Dusty's face.

"Did a sheriff's office put this out, Captain Fog?" he asked, a touch nervously.

"You fixing to try for the reward, *mister?*" growled the Kid.

From the emphasis placed upon the last word, plus a knowledge that no Texan said "mister" after learning one's name if he liked the person he addressed, warned Caldwell that he had committed something in the nature of a *fau pax*.

Not only the Kid, but Doc—who Caldwell owed so much—stood glaring coldly.

"Of course not," he replied quickly. "I just thought——"

"No sheriff's office put it out," Dusty said, his voice quiet and friendly. "There's no description or picture of me for one thing. More important, there's nothing to say where to collect the bounty."

Taking the paper, Caldwell looked at it and found that Dusty told the truth. While he could not claim to be an authority on such matters, his curiosity had led him to study a number of wanted posters displayed outside post offices and other such places in the towns through which the wagons passed. In every case, even without a picture—either an artist's impression or a photograph—the poster bore a description and notification of where the reward money could be collected on fulfilling the terms stated. Another small thing struck Caldwell about the paper he held. On almost every other he saw, the wording read, *WANTED DEAD OR ALIVE,* or *WANTED ALIVE*. None that he could remember carried the cryptic, somehow chilling terms printed on the sheet he held.

"I see," Caldwell remarked.

"Each law enforcement office puts out its own dodgers on wanted men," Dusty explained, guessing that Caldwell made a stock reply without really understanding the implications. "How they word the poster depends on what the man is wanted for. Say he got away with a fair amount of money, or something recoverable, then the dodger would say, 'Wanted Alive.' Dead he couldn't do any talking. Then the office that put out the dodger tells the world about it. That's so any peace officer who gets the man knows who to notify. Or so that any bounty hunter who picks up the wanted man can tell where he gets his pay."

At that time there was no central police organization in the United States; no official body with country-wide jurisdiction or records office to act as a central gathering point for such details. The United States marshals handled only federal matters and for the most part left local law enforcement to the county or municipal authorities involved. While the Secret Service could come and go all through the country, their duties involved national security and handling counterfeiting. For the rest, each county had its own sheriff's office and in addition any big town maintained its own police force in the form of the town marshal's office. The extent of co-operation between municipal and county authorities varied, as did the standard of efficiency of the local law. When putting out a wanted poster, the issuer guaranteed to pay a certain sum of money as reward. While any county sheriff or town marshal could act as witness to the *bona fides* of a claimant for the reward, only the office which put out the dodger would pay the money. So a wanted poster always told who put it out.

"How did that cowhand come to be carrying it?" Caldwell inquired.

"Now that's a good question," Dusty drawled. "Only none of that bunch were cowhands."

"If any of them ever worked cattle, it wouldn't be for the man who laid the brand on it," Doc agreed, kneeling by the wounded hard-case and ripping up his shirt sleeve to expose the wound.

"Could try to get him talking again," the Kid suggested, nodding to the victim of his rifle.

"When I start telling you how to read sign, you can show me how to doctor," Doc answered. "If you damned Comanches'd-stop——"

"Choke off," Dusty ordered. "The way I see it, that bunch were passing, saw the wagons, figured you for easy meat and came in to take anything they needed."

"Eight of them riding together," the Kid drawled. "They'd be heading to some fuss. Only I've not heard of any big enough to want that many hired guns."

"They might have come from some local ranch," Caldwell said.

"The nearest's thirty miles off," Dusty answered. "And

they were travelling. A man doesn't tote along his thirty-year gatherings when he's out riding for a spread. All that bunch had filled bedrolls on their saddles."

While speaking, Dusty watched the two men assigned to help the Kid dispose of the body. One of them had taken a blanket and covered the gory shape on the ground. Now they stood waiting for further orders. Dusty let them wait, wanting the Kid on hand until they thrashed the matter out.

"They were headed for some trouble," the Kid stated.

"Could have been riding away after helping finish some," Caldwell suggested.

"That's possible, but not likely," Dusty replied. "Word about gun-trouble spreads like fire across dry grass, and we've heard nothing."

"Perhaps the trouble was a long way off."

"It'd have to be a long way for word not to spread. And if they had been paid off, they'd not likely be riding in a bunch. Hired guns don't make many friends even among their own kind, and there's precious few of them would trust each other when carrying pay from some fuss."

"Might they be outlaws on their way to a robbery?" asked Caldwell.

"Could be," Dusty admitted. "There are some hired guns who mix robbery with taking pay for fighting. But that doesn't explain how they come to be carrying this damned paper."

"That is strange," Caldwell agreed.

"Strange isn't the word I'd put to it," Dusty said.

"Or me," grunted the Kid.

"It couldn't just be a joke?"

Before either Dusty or the Kid—Doc being fully engrossed with his work and ignoring the others—could reply to Caldwell's suggestion, they saw two riders appear in the distance. While the Eastern-bred man could make out only a pair of dots on the horizon, the Kid made a correct identification instantly and Dusty only a short time later.

"Mark and Waco," Dusty said.

"Coming up like it was feed time," confirmed the Kid. "Or like there was a pretty gal waiting here—or a father out with his scattergun back at Junction."

"Could the poster be a joke, Captain Fog?" Caldwell persisted.

Ten minutes later he received his answer and knew that the poster was no joke; or if aimed to be, had brought about near tragic results.

"Damned fool kid," Dusty drawled. "Did you telegraph to home and tell them I'm still all right, Mark?"

"Thought it'd be best," the blond giant answered.

Knowing the almost uncanny manner in which news could spread over the range country, Mark wasted no time in visiting Junction City's Wells Fargo office and dispatching a message to Dusty's parents in Polveroso City, Texas, informing them that rumors of their son's death were untrue. The wisdom of the action showed when word reached Rio Hondo county, only three days after the incident in Junction City, that Dusty had been killed by a knife over on the Arizona-New Mexico line.

"Reckon that bunch were looking for you, Dusty?" asked Waco.

"I don't think so," Dusty replied. "They didn't come in like they expected any trouble."

"Happen paleface medicineman don't kill him off," drawled the Kid. "We've got us a gent here who knows all the answers."

Doc gave a sniff and answered, "Way you're shooting 'em these days, a first-year student could cure them."

However he knew from his examination that the man had been exceptionally lucky. Knowing the Kid, Doc did not for a moment believe the bullet had been aimed to make such a fancy hit. With Dusty's life at stake, the Kid would not waste time in taking the careful aim necessary to send a bullet so it merely carved a slice out of the under-side of the hard-case's arm.

A couple of inches higher and the man would never have

used his arm again. While the forty grain powder charge of the Winchester '73 might be light as far as rifle loads went, the conformation of the bullet made it a wicked weapon to use against men. Early in the rifle's development it had been discovered that the mixture of a sharp-pointed, centerfire bullet and a tubular magazine invited trouble. A hard knock might send the point of the bullet ramming into the primer cap of the round ahead in the tube magazine and cause a premature detonation, damaging the gun beyond repair. To overcome the failing, Winchester cut off the point of the bullet to leave a flat surface larger than the circumference of the primer cap. While this effectively prevented premature discharge, it also gave the bullet a terrible mushroom on impact. Much in the same way as a dum-dum bullet, the flat-nosed .44.40 round did little damage at its point of entry but spread out in a funnel-like manner once inside.

Working fast, for he had delayed almost to the limits of safety, Doc cleaned the wound, stopped the flow of blood and examined the damage. Although very painful and almost touching the bone, no permanent damage ought to come from the wound. Using clean white cloth brought by the woman who helped with the delivery of Caldwell's child, Doc bandaged the wound and strapped it to the man's side to keep it immobile. Even as he completed his work, Doc felt the man stirring and heard groans which told of approaching consciousness.

"He'll do," the slim Texan stated, rising and turning to Dusty.

Knowing Doc's temper tended to be a mite touchy when engaged in such work, the other members of the floating outfit had withdrawn and waited for permission before coming close once more.

"Do we talk to him now?" asked the Kid mildly, but there was no mildness in his eyes.

Directing a questioning glance at Doc, Dusty caught a shake of the head and replied, "Leave him come out of it first, Mark, get him into the shade and have water fetched for him. Waco, go take the supplies to the folk who ordered them, then head down to the river and bring in the horses closer to camp."

"Yo!" answered the youngster and departed.

"Lon, see to the burying."

"I thought you'd forgot all about that," grunted the Kid.

"I'll just bet you did," Dusty grinned. "Don't take all day. I want us all on hand when we hold some talk with that *hombre*."

By the time Waco and the Kid returned from handling their work, the wounded man—who claimed the unimaginative name of Brown—had recovered sufficiently to sit up. Resting his back against the wheel of one of the wagons, he watched with a sense of foreboding as the Texans gathered in a half circle before him. At Dusty's request, the people of the train went about their business and left his men to deal with Brown. Only Caldwell, something of a student of human nature, hovered in the background.

Brown wondered what might be due to happen to him. While nobody had mentioned the matter, he felt sure that they must have found the wanted poster and figured they would want some questions answered.

"Why'd you come here?" asked Dusty.

Staring up at the grim-faced Texans, Brown ran his tongue-tip across lips which suddenly felt very dry. "For a meal."

"Where're you going?"

"Was going with Baines, him you shot, Cap'n Fog."

"Where to?"

"I don't know."

"Hombre!" snapped the Ysabel Kid. "You can do it hard or easy, but we aim to have us some answers. It's all one to me how we get 'em."

"But not to me," objected Doc. "I wasted time patching this cuss up."

"I don't know where he was taking us!" yelped Brown.

"So help me, that's the living truth. I'd been over in New Mexico, just earning eating money, when I met up with Baines. He'd got something on, needed a few boys to handle it, so I took on."

"Without knowing where you'd be going, or why?" said Dusty sceptically.

"He paid out twenty bucks a man. What'd I to lose?"

"Who put the bounty on my scalp?"

The question came as something of a shock and Brown did not have the presence of mind to think up a satisfactory lie. "Wh-what bounty?"

"Don't fuss us, *hombre!*" growled the Kid, Comanche-mean and scowling down. "We all know a heap of ways to make a man unhappy."

"Sure," agreed Mark, idly snapping his clenched right fist into the palm of the left hand. "Now me, I always reckon working on the nose makes a man talk best."

Out came Waco's right hand Colt in a casual flicker of movement, pin-wheeling on an educated forefinger, slapping staghorn grips into his palm and the thumb easing back the hammer. Almost gently he laid the gun's .45 muzzle on the man's nose end. "It sure does," he drawled. "Or I could stand off a few yards and shoot holes in his ears. They always talk when I do that."

"Unless you miss and put the bullet between their eyes," Doc commented. "I like to work close up. Go fetch me my doctoring tools, boy, and I'll show you how to extract answers like teeth."

Anticipation of what would come had always formed a major part in the success of any such campaign. Once in the war, Dusty had seen the rebel spy, Belle Boyd, obtain information from a captured Yankee agent by using much the same technique. Since then he had handled interrogations in a similar manner when working as a lawman. Everything depended on whether the one being treated believed his captors intended to carry out the threats.

Watching the Texans' faces. Brown did not for a moment doubt that any refusal to co-operate would bring painful results. Nothing in the Ysabel Kid's past history hinted that he, for one, possessed any great scruples when dealing with an unco-operative enemy. Brown wondered how he ever thought that dark, savage, Comanche face looked young and innocent.

"You wouldn't allow them to torture this man, Captain Fog," Caldwell put in.

"Well, now," Dusty replied, pleased that the other interrupted. "That all depends."

"Upon what?"

"Whether he tells us what we want to know, or not."

"But he's wounded!" Caldwell protested.

"Which same we never asked him to get that way," Mark pointed out.

"All he has to do is talk and we don't want hide nor hair of him," the Kid continued.

"Might even call it payment for my medical services," Doc went on.

"Comes to a real smart point, mister," drawled Waco, turning to Caldwell. "There's no way you can stop us doing it."

Which Caldwell had to admit was all too true. He might be a young man with ideals, but doubted if any of his fellow travellers attained such high standards. None of them would go against the Texans to help a man who had been part of a bunch planning to rob them.

Without realising it, Caldwell had helped Dusty by his attempted interference. Maybe Brown hoped for intervention by the dudes. If so, he now knew that no such aid could be expected.

Caldwell opened his mouth to speak, then gave thought to Doc's words. Not only Brown owed the slim, pallid Texan a debt for medical services received. Looking at Dusty's party, Caldwell felt puzzled at the change in their ways. No longer did they act like a bunch of cheerful school-boys, but stood grim, cold, menacing. Somehow such a change did not seem to be in character—although clearly the point escaped the scared-looking hard-case.

"What do you want to know?" croaked Brown.

"Where that reward dodger came from," Dusty answered.

"I don't know where Baines picked his up from—and that's the gospel truth, Cap'n. But I've seen them in more than one place."

"What kind of place?"

"Saloons, our hang-outs, different stations along the Out-law Trail. They've been well spread over the past few weeks."

Dusty nodded at the confirmation of his thoughts on the affair. In every major town throughout the West, at least one saloon served as headquarters and hang-out for profes-sional gun fighters. Such places acted as gathering points, information collectors and employment bureaus for men who sold their skill with a gun. Anybody who knew where to look could contact hired killers of varying ability by visiting one of the hang-outs. While not all hired guns were outlaws, many augmented their earnings in lean times by riding on robberies; so it seemed likely that Brown would know the Outlaw Trail. Running from the Canadian line, through Landusky, Montana, down via Wyoming's Buffalo, Kaycee and Hole-In-The-Wall country, to Robbers' Roost and Brown's Hole in Utah, on, curving from north-east Arizona, across the line and down into Mexico via the south-west edge of New Mexico, the Outlaw Trail had along its length many places where wanted men could gather, ex-change news and be safe from the law. Word and the posters could be passed along the Outlaw Trail with the certainty of it spreading rapidly and where it would do most good.

"That poster didn't say where to go for the bounty," Waco said. "Now me, I'd say that'd be the first thing any-body fool enough to try for it'd want to know."

"Word had it that the man who got Cap'n Fog should

ought to take his gunbelt to Pasear Hennessey's place down on the Mexican border."

"Do you know it, Lon?" asked Dusty.

"He's got two places," replied the Kid, whose smuggling up-bringing gave him an encyclopaedic knowledge of the Mexican border country. "One on an island in the Rio Grande and the other at the south end of the Outlaw Trail. Now happen this gent can tell us which one——"

"The one on the Trail," yelped Brown, hot and eager to appear helpful.

"Thanks," Dusty said.

"I'd thank you myself," purred the Kid, his bowie knife sliding from its sheath. "Only I know you're lying in your teeth. Not even Pasear's own mother'd be hawg-stupid enough to leave him to hold five thousand dollars of real money."

"I'm not lying, Kid!" wailed Brown. "All I know is, the feller who gets Cap'n Fog has to take the gunbelt as proof he done it and Pasear'll tell him where to go to collect."

"Do we call on Mr. Hennessey, Dusty?" asked Waco.

"And leave the remuda out here?" smiled the small Texan.

"Take them back with us'd strike some as the answer," sniffed the youngster.

"Then 'some' ought to know that Colonel Raines wants those horses urgently, boy," Mark pointed out.

"Happen you three could handle the remuda, me and the boy could take it," the Kid suggested.

"Neither of them do any work anyways," Mark drawled. "Why'd we miss 'em?"

Knowing that the Kid would not ask for Waco's assistance unless the matter could be handled without it, Dusty gave his agreement to the request.

"All right," he said. "Take him. Need anything else?"

"Four of the best hosses in the remuda to ride relay— and rifle shells."

"How many?"

"All you can spare," the Kid said quietly.

"I've a full box I can let you have," Mark offered.

"Gracias," answered the Kid. "How about you, Doc?"

"Damned if I don't buy a Centennial," Doc growled. "That way only the boy'll be able to bum shells off me."

On a visit to Chicago, Waco had purchased one of the latest rifles to leave the Winchester factory.* With a calibre of .45.75, the rifle first appeared at the Philadelphia Centennial Exposition and was the company's answer to the heavy calibre, single-shot rifles of the day Taking a much larger bullet than its predecessor, the rounds could not be interchanged. However, Waco brought along a good supply of ammunition in the hope of sampling the hunting around Backsight and giving the rifle a thorough shooting trial.

Despite his comments, Doc went straight off to collect the ammunition. He saw that Dusty and Mark both contributed their share to the sum total and this puzzled him. Knowing that the Kid never travelled without at least a hundred rounds for his rifle along, Doc felt puzzled. Taken with his normal supply, the Kid now had getting on for two hundred and fifty bullets. A tolerable amount when one remembered that he hit more times than missed when using that magnificent rifle.

Dusty and Mark had much the same thoughts as Doc, but all knew better than waste time in asking questions. On their arrival, the scout had cancelled his rush to Junction City and taken the opportunity to go out on a meat-hunting expedition. When he returned, the Texans planned to move on with the herd of blood stock for delivery to the ranch of Colonel Raines. Until that time they had work to do, preparing Waco and the Kid for a long, hard and fast ride to Pasear Hennessey's place. Riding relay, two such horsemasters as the Kid and Waco could cover the one hundred and fifty miles to Pasear Hennessey's place in just over two

*Told in *Waco's Debt*.

days. How long their business took depended on Hennessey's willingness to co-operate, then they would have to make the best possible time north to rejoin Dusty at Backsight.

Working with the skill of long practice, Mark and Dusty cut out four of the best horses from the remuda. Colonel Raines would understand the necessity when told and make no complaints. By riding alternately on the two horses and their personal mount the Kid and Waco would be able to travel much faster than would be possible using one horse.

After collecting and saddling his huge, wild-looking white stallion, the Kid looked to where Waco led up one of the relay—the paint having been pushed hard during the ride from Junction City.

"You got all you need, Lon?" asked Dusty.

"Everything," agreed the Kid, sliding his rifle into the saddle-boot. "All right, let's go make talk with Pasear Hennessey."

CHAPTER FIVE

The Wild Onion Crew

The noonday silence of Backsight was suddenly shattered by the thunder of hooves, wild cowboy yells and the crack of shots as half a dozen riders tore along Main Street in the direction of the Arizona State Saloon.

Standing at the window of the Bismai Cafe, Maisie Randel watched the newcomers with first tolerant amusement, then growing concern as she saw the complete disregard the party showed for the property or persons of the citizens. One of the cowhands turned his horse; rode it on to the sidewalk and charged along to the detriment of the few pedestrians who used what ought to have been a safe footpath. On seeing a man and woman take hurried leaps into the ladies' wear shop that had taken over the premises left vacant by Dusty Fog's smashing of the Considine bunch—in which Maisie, then a Pinkerton operative, took a major part—she turned and called across towards the kitchen.

"Biscuits!"

Having already heard the ruckus in the street, Maisie's husband stepped into the dining-room, leaving his supervision of the evening's menu. Biscuits Randel stood almost six foot three and had heft to match it. Genial featured most of the time, he did not show it as he joined and towered over his wife. Since leaving the Pinkerton service, Maisie had changed little. Mousey blonde hair, neatly coiffured, framed a good-looking, merry face that could become grim and determined when necessary. Good food and a settled life had filled out her frame in a plump, attractive manner. Healthy exercise and hard work kept the plumpness firm flesh and under the spotlessly clean gingham dress she curved in at the waist naturally. Maisie could claim to be as shapely a woman as any in town even though in her middle thirties.

"Not the Lazy O, Bradded R, nor yet Leyland's," Biscuits stated, studying the riders. "Swede Larsen's boys were only in two days back."

"I did hear that somebody had bought the old Fernandez place," Maisie replied. "Look at that!"

Screeching with excitement, one of the riders drew his Colt and threw four shots in the direction of a water-filled barrel, the property of the town's Volunteer Fire Department, which stood at the edge of the sidewalk. Only two of the bullets struck the comparatively harmless side of the barrel, a foolish enough action as the water inside was ready for use in case of a fire, the remaining lead missed and tore furrows in the sidewalk.

"Reckon I'll just have to go out there and have words with 'em," said Biscuits mildly. "Seem to know a couple of them."

"Two of them worked for Larsen until he changed horses in their string," Maisie answered. "The tall one trying to grow a moustache was out at Leyland's until the Major fired him and threatened to set him afoot."

"As bad as that, boss-gal?"

"Idle as they come, and a trouble maker. I'll just fetch it for you, dear."

Watching Maisie act the dutiful wife by going to fetch her husband his tools before dispatching him to work, Biscuits grinned. Until four years ago Maisie had never been west of the Pecos; to his knowledge, for they rarely discussed her work with Pinkertons. Yet there she stood, talking in range terms. When the boss of a ranch changed a horse in one of his hand's string of work mounts, it was taken that the cowboy had out-stayed his welcome and if he had any sense, he quit. Only on the most extreme provocation would a rancher set a discharged hand afoot, leave him without a horse. In the range country folks said, "A man afoot is no man at all," and in a cowhand's case that proved all too true. Should the hand discharged not own a horse for any reason, the rancher mostly allowed him to use one of the remuda as transportation to his next employment. Setting a man afoot was regarded as so serious that such an affair rarely ended without lead flying.

By the time Biscuits had pinned the tarnished star in his shirt, Maisie returned to hand him his favourite pacification instrument; a twenty inch barrelled Greener ten gauge shotgun of the style favoured by Wells Fargo express messengers and guards.

"Take care now," Maisie warned as Biscuits walked to the door.

"Don't I always?" grinned her husband and left the building.

Ever since his old friend and business rival left the Alamo Saloon and went out to California, Eddy Last found life irksome. True he made more money as owner of Backsight's only remaining saloon, but that did not make up for the lack of leisure caused by the extra customers. No longer could the lean, mournful-looking Last look forward to lounging at the bar and dispensing wisdom to his cronies of an evening. Instead he found himself constantly badgered by some pesky customer who wanted serving and was not well enough known to be told to go pour it himself.

One way and another, even though alone in the bar-room, it could not be claimed that Last felt any great delight at seeing the six riders pass one of the big front windows, or hear them halt outside. From what he had heard during the newcomers' ride through town, he reckoned they might be more trouble than trade. Experienced in his work, Last knew and regarded tolerantly the wildness cowhands often showed on entering town. Way he figured it, men working the long hours cowhands normally did had a right to play a mite wild and rough when they received their pay. So he expected horseplay, the occasional rough-house, and even some judicious indoor target practice. Last felt puzzled as he heard boots pounding the sidewalk towards his doors. For the most part the local cowhands behaved within reasonable bounds, knowing that Biscuits Randel took his duties as town marshal seriously and objected to too violent fooling.

Studying the six young men as they crowded into the room, Last scowled and his puzzlement grew. To the best of his knowledge none were employed on the local ranches, although three had been at one time. Clearly all had been drinking on their way into town and reached that state when truculent good humor seemed the only attitude.

Laughing, talking in loud voices, jostling each other, the six young men headed for the bar. A tall, sullen-faced, though handsome young man with curly black hair appeared to be the ringleader. Low-tied at his right side hung a shining Colt with mock pearl handles, far from which, when he remembered, his hand never moved. There walked trouble, or Last had never seen it; the kind who got himself a reputation of being a hard man, or died real sudden when meeting someone he did not impress. The rest seemed to be the kind that gave all cowhands a bad name among town folks. Disinclined to work, they held down a riding job as long as a boss tolerated them, did as little as possible and could be found at the core of every cowhand disturbance.

"Set 'em up, Grandpappy," ordered the leader. "It's your buy, Mick."

Although clearly not caring for the suggestion, the one addressed dug into his pocket and tossed down money. Last produced a bottle of whisky and started pouring into glasses.

"Hey, where's the gals?" the leader demanded, looking around him as he rat-holed four fingers of raw frontier whisky.

"Not in yet," Last replied. Another objection he had towards the growth of the town and sudden prosperity had been having to employ girls to help entertain his customers. While Last believed in taking his drinking seriously, the local hands demanded female company when celebrating.

"Who do we dance with then?" asked the leader.

"Old Billy here sure is a dancing fool," whooped the drink-buyer.

"I sure am," the leader agreed. "And if there's no gals to dance with; why you can come out here and dance for us, Grandpappy."

"Can't say as I take to being called Grandpappy by you, my kids all having more sense than sire you," Last growled. "And I sure as hell can't see me dancing."

"Maybe you won't have any choice," Billy snarled, all vestiges of fun leaving him. "What kind of a one-hoss town is this, gone noon and no gals."

"Town looks as good going out as coming in," Last answered. "Same as this place. I'm rich enough not to miss your custom."

"Are, huh?" Billy snarled and picked up the bottle, throwing it in the direction of the big bar mirror.

While knowing that to do so would provoke trouble, Last still acted. Up shot his right hand, catching the bottle. Then he heaved it back, straight at the cowhand's head. Billy yelled and ducked hurriedly, feeling the bottle scrape his ear in passing, and staggering back in his surprise at Last's unexpected action.

"Get the bastard!" he screeched and hurled himself towards the bar.

A Merwin and Hulbert Army Pocket revolver lay on a shelf under the bar, but slightly too far away from Last for him to reach it in time. Besides, he figured flashing a firearm at that time might lead to shooting. So as Billy leapt up, meaning to go over the bar and land on his enemy, Last shot out his right hand. A bartender learned many things beyond the mere serving of drinks, including how to handle awkward customers. Hard knuckles smashed into Billy's face and flung him back from the bar to sprawl on the floor.

Even as their self-appointed leader lit down, nose and mouth bleeding, the remainder of the party decided to take a hand. Clenching their fists, two of them headed towards the end of the bar, thinking to take a less risky route to their victim. All the remaining trio hurled their glasses across the bar, but fortunately missed the mirror. Not that their efforts went unrewarded. Two whisky bottles burst as the glasses struck them and the third shattered on a calendar put out by a whisky distillery.

"All right, boys," said a sleepy voice from the front door. "Fun's over. Time to pay for it now."

Turning, the youngsters found themselves confronted by the bulky shape of the town marshal. He slouched forward, looking as slow and awkward as a white-jawed, mossy-horned old bull buffalo waiting for the wolves to pick it off; the Greener seeming almost small in his big right hand.

Billy came to his feet, rubbed a hand across his face, looked at the red smear on it and snarled a curse. Then, thinking of his public image—even though the term had not yet come into use and he knew nothing of such things— Billy moved a couple of paces forward to block Biscuit's path.

"That's far enough, John Law," he warned.

"Reckon you didn't hear me, boy," Biscuits answered, continuing his steady advance. "I said the fun's over."

"Now me," Billy replied, watching the big right hand for the first sign of it beginning to lift the shotgun into a firing position, "I thought it'd just now started."

Legs braced apart, knees slightly bent, fingers spread over the Colt's butt, Billy faced the advancing Biscuits—

and made two prime errors in tactics due to his lack of practical experience. First, he telegraphed his intentions by adopting such a stance; a trained gun fighter would never have given such a warning. Secondly, he kept his eyes on Biscuit's right hand and allowed the marshal to come in far too close.

Suddenly Billy realised his danger and reached towards his gun. For a big, lethargic-looking man, Biscuits could move with some speed. Instead of raising the shotgun, the marshal swung his big left hand in a slap that caught Billy alongside the head and spun him around to crash into the three young men who threw the glasses, effectively preventing them from taking any action.

Halting, the remaining pair tried to decide what they should do. Before either reached any decision, Last made the required few steps along the bar and produced an answer to their problems."

"Just stand there, boys," he ordered, lining the Merwin in their direction.

Raising his shotgun so as to catch the foregrip in his left hand, Biscuits threw down on the tangle of young men and ended any hostile moves they might have figured on making. Being mindful of the truth in the old saying, "There's always a burying with buckshot," the young men discarded the idea of resistance.

"Who'd you bunch ride for?" Randel asked when all movement ceased.

"The Whangdoodle," Mick answered sullenly.

"Which same there's not one around these parts," grunted the marshal. "You can do better'n that."

"It's the old Fernandez place," explained one of the trio who had worked locally "Miss Benedict bought it and took us on."

"She shows mighty poor judgement," Biscuits said. "Shed the gunbelts, you can cool off for a spell in the pokey."

"For hoorawing the town?" yelped Billy.

"For riding to the public's danger, creating a disturbance, reckless discharging of firearms within city limits, damage to property," intoned Biscuits. "Which same we don't figure on having them sort of monkey-shines in Backsight."

"Maybe you never had a man who could do 'em," snarled Billy, his head still singing and throbbing from the slap.

"Or maybe we never had nobody fool enough to try," answered Biscuits. "And I don't aim to keep asking about them belts."

Slowly, reluctantly, the young men discarded their gun-belts. Asking Last to gather up the arms and bring them to the jail, Biscuits escorted the discomforted cowhands from the building. On the street a small bunch of citizens watched with approval. Most, if not all, drew a considerable portion of their livelihood from the local cowhands and there was little of the antipathy between the two groups found in some towns. However there were well-defined limits to what the citizens would tolerate in cowhand behavior and the six had passed well beyond the limits during their reckless, foolish dash into town.

Biscuits might—and frequently did—claim he was no law-man, but he knew his work. If he had allowed the breach to pass, it would have encouraged more of the same. The time to show tolerance and leniency was after the recipients proved worthy of it. After a spell in jail and a stiff fine, the Whangdoodle's crew would think twice before making trouble in town again.

While escorting his prisoners to the jail, Biscuits saw a rider approaching Main Street along the rough trail to the south-west. He observed the newcomer to be a woman, noted she rode astride and that he could not place her as a local resident. Wanting to get the young men off the street, he wasted no time in idle conjecture; although the direction from which she came gave him a clue as to her identity.

The town of Backsight did not run to hiring more than one peace officer, so Biscuits tended to the placing of his prisoners in the cells which lay behind the main office of the building. After locking the barred door, he returned to the main office and heard a horse halt outside. Leather creaked as the rider dismounted and feet thudded lightly across the porch. The office door opened to admit Myra Considine. Standing by his desk, Biscuits looked the girl over. Taking in her silk shirt waist, doeskin divided skirt and fancy boots, he next studied her head. Red hair, cut fairly short—the black tresses at the penitentiary had been a wig—peeked from under a black Stetson, framing a face which struck Biscuits as being vaguely familiar.

"Howdy, ma'am," he greeted cordially.

"My name is Benedict," she answered, her voice cold. "Did I see you bringing some of my men in here?"

"Reckon you did, ma'am," the marshal agreed.

"On what charge were they arrested?"

"Shucks. Wasn't thinking of making any charges at all."

"Then by what right are you holding them?"

"Just figured they'd be a whole heap better happen they had time to cool down a mite, ma'am. See, they'd been hoorawing the town something wild and I figured to show them how we handle things here in Backsight, them being strangers."

"The law should be the same for everyone, not a matter of length of residence," Myra snorted.

"I'd've done the same no matter who they was," Biscuits answered. "Those boys're trouble, ma'am, real wild. Three of them's been fired from spreads hereabouts for it."

"So I understood when I hired them," Myra informed him coldly. "I took them on to give them a second chance and allow them to show that they could behave well."

"Wouldn't want to say they'd done that, way they come in today, ma'am," Biscuits stated.

"Just high spirits!" the girl snorted, watching Biscuit's face all the time. "But recognising three of them, you immediately threw them into jail. I warn you, marshal, I will not tolerate victimization."

During the time her brother and sister built a considerable

fortune in a variety of crooked deals, Myra had been in college back East; one of the progressive kind which accepted women students. There she joined the Radical Republican movement and from them learned the value of the word "victimization" when dealing with law enforcement officers. Unfortunately for her—although the community as a whole benefited by it—Arizona had not come under the sway of such noble people and not even a Republican newspaper showed misguided sympathy for law-breakers. So Biscuits failed to show terror at the dreaded word.

"Can't say as there'll be any, ma'am," he remarked calmly. "Folks hereabouts get on well with the cowhands, most times, but a few fool tricks like that bunch pulled could spoil it all."

"Did they behave badly?"

"Well now, that depends on what *you'd* call badly, ma'am. Came charging in here like the Sioux after General Custer. One of 'em near to rode down a man and his wife—on the sidewalk. Another threw lead kind of wild, punctured a couple of holes in one of them barrels we keep filled in case of fire. Country's kind of dry these days. Place gets on fire, we need it dousing quick and that takes water. Two other bullets ploughed up the sidewalk, which didn't hurt it none. Only they could have done bad damage. Then they started a ruckus down at the saloon. Like I said, it all depends on what *you* call behaving bad."

"It could all have been sheer high spirits," Myra commented, having an uneasy feeling that the interview had slipped away from her.

"There's a difference between high spirits and plumb ornery meanness, ma'am. We don't mind hosses galloping in town, but they've got to be kept off the sidewalks. Any shooting's got to be straight up in the air, that way only the birds or angels get hurt. You're new to the West?"

"I am."

"Was I you, I'd get rid of that bunch. They're trouble.

Happen you keep 'em on, you'll get the name for running a wild onion crew. Decent hands'll steer clear of you and only other yahoos like them pack'll take on. I never yet saw a wild-onion bunch that wasn't trouble to everybody, including their boss."

"I'll bear it in mind," Myra promised. "And what of my men?"

"They'll have to pay for the damage they've done and a fine for the trouble they put me to, then be let out when they've cooled down."

"Will seventy dollars cover it?"

"I reckon so, fines included," Biscuits agreed.

"Then I'll pay right now," she said and reached towards her skirt's pocket.

"There's no need for that, ma'am," Biscuits objected. "I'll take a collection from among 'em. Hurts more that way, hits them in the pockets and makes them less likely to do it again."

"No. I'll pay and deduct it from their wages."

"You'll have to take the money to Counsellor Gimzewski's office," Biscuits put in. "He acts as justice of the peace and handles them things."

"Couldn't you——" she began.

"No, ma'am!" replied Biscuits, all the lethargy leaving him and a cold, warning expression coming to his face.

"No offense," Myra hastened to say. "I thought it might save time."

"That's what I thought you thought, ma'am," answered Biscuits. "You can't miss the counsellor's office. It's next door to the Wells Fargo office, got his shingle hanging on it."

Turning, Myra walked from the room. Her trip to town had not been wasted, nor had the bottle of whisky handed to the six men as they left the ranch. Wishing to study the opposition, she sent the six cowhands on ahead and knew how they would behave on their arrival. On her first sight of Biscuits, she took him for a dull-witted hulk hired for muscle alone—a mistake more than one person made. After a few moments conversation she knew her first impression to be wrong. A smart working brain operated in that big sleepy-looking head. The attempt at bribery, a spontaneous action, came to nothing. If the marshal had accepted her offer of an unofficial settlement, it would have opened the way for other such arrangements. Myra now knew that a smart, incorruptible man held office; which would necessitate a slight change in her plans.

Biscuits watched the girl ride in the direction of the justice of the peace's office and rubbed a hand over his close-cropped head.

"Now who is it she puts me in mind of?" he mused.

CHAPTER SIX

Dusty Fog Is Coming Here

The man who had called himself Father Donglar drew a white silk shirt down over his sweat-slicked body and breathed heavily. While he enjoyed the company of women, he could not help thinking that his present situation carried things a mite too far.

Of course, if it came to a point, he had only himself to blame, he ruefully—if silently—admitted. Myra's behavior ought to have given him a warning of what to expect from the distaff side of the Considine family. In fact, most men would have been more than satisfied with just her and steered clear of an entanglement elsewhere.

Not Donglar. He possessed the kind of ego that must make a stab at conquering any good-looking woman who came his way. Three days after the escape of Anthea Considine, disregarding the fact that he already carried on a surreptitious romance with Myra, he made his move and ensnared the elder sister. They had been staying at a ranch, the owner of which made more money hiding folk on the run than out of his cattle, and Myra went into town to pick up the latest news of moves to recapture Anthea. Ten minutes after Myra rode out, Anthea and Donglar lay on the bed in his room, and he learned that it ran in the family.

From then on Donglar found himself conducting two separate affairs, and struggling desperately to prevent either of the female participants learning of his interest in the other. Having put much time and effort into freeing Anthea, he wanted to see a return for his services—and not the kind handed out so freely by both sisters. In addition to taking her revenge on the people of Backsight, Anthea proposed to make a large sum of money. Donglar hoped to see a fair share of the profits coming his way. So he worked hard at persuading both girls that each must keep the other from becoming jealous and act as if nothing tender existed between her and him.

The scheme worked, although it grew daily more difficult to keep the true state of affairs hidden. It also proved a mighty exhausting business, satisfying the demands of a pair of lusty girls like the Considine sisters.

"Why the rush to leave, Charles?" asked Anthea, sprawled on the bed.

Turning he looked at her. Without her clothes, the hard firmness of her body showed to its best effect. A leather sheath strapped around her forearm, hiding the scar left by Maisie Randel's bullet on the day Dusty Fog killed her brother and ended their evil schemes.

"Myra ought to be back from town soon," he warned. "It wouldn't do for her to see me coming out of your bedroom."

"Why not?" Anthea hissed. "She'll know about us soon enough when we announce our engagement. And I don't see why we shouldn't do that as soon as she comes back."

"You don't, huh?"

"No, I don't. We can manage without her."

"And who'll meet visitors from town, act as a front for you?" Donglar snorted. "Those folk in Backsight, at least some of them, won't have forgotten what you look like. They'd recognise you. So we need Myra here."

"She's beginning to annoy me, the way she keeps pawing

you," Anthea answered. "I don't see why——"

"I've told you why. Myra's only young and if she gets annoyed she might spoil the whole game."

"I suppose you're right," Anthea sniffed. "But stay away from her, Charles."

Before Donglar could think up an answer, they heard hooves drumming outside. Crossing to the window, Donglar carefully eased back one side of the curtains and looked down. With something like relief, he saw that the riders below were not Myra and the cowhands she took to town.

"It looks like some of the guns we need have just arrived," he said. "I can't see Baines with them, but his pard, Coffee's there. You'd better stay up here and out of sight while I go and deal with them."

"Don't I get a kiss before you go?" Anthea purred, rising and walking across the room in the man's direction.

At that moment Donglar seriously considered becoming a Trappist monk. After almost a solid hour of varied love-making, he could barely raise any enthusiasm or desire for more. However, having seen something of the Considine temper when crossed, he wished to avoid any discord. Taking Anthea in his arms, he kissed her and felt her arms lock around him, crushing and digging fingers into his flesh. At last he managed to free himself and escape from the room.

"Whew!" he gasped, mopping his face and heading for the stairs. "There must be easier ways of earning a dollar."

In its day, the big house had belonged to a Mexican *haciendero*, being the winter residence used to escape the heat of the southern range. Fernandez took little care of the building during his brief period of occupation and it had been left untouched since his death at the hands of Dusty Fog. However, on first being approached by Myra, almost a year before, Donglar saw the advantages of such a base for operations. The property lay in Coconino County and went cheap to defray the loss of taxes it incurred. Avoiding Backsight, so as to escape notice, Donglar imported servants and had the place made habitable.

Walking down the wide flight of stairs, he decided that he had done his work well. The house would make a jim-dandy home and was the kind of place he always dreamed of owning. If it did not have the disadvantage of containing the two Considine sisters—however, time might offer him a cure for that.

On crossing the big entrance hall, he pushed open the main doors and stepped on to the porch. The six men in the act of dismounting threw interested glances in Donglar's direction and he studied them, gauging their quality.

"Where's Baines?" he demanded, looking at the short, stocky man whose panic had caused the hurried departure from the wagon train.

"He won't be coming back."

"Why not, Coffee?"

"He's dead."

"And how did he die?" growled Donglar.

"We ran into some fuss back towards the New Mexico line and a Texan made wolf bait of old Baines," Coffee explained, then to avert the wrath which he expected. "There'll be nothing come of it."

"Tell me what happened," ordered Donglar.

Knowing something of the way of the handsome man before him, Coffee started into an account of the hectic visit to the small wagon train. In doing so, he tried to put himself and his companions in as good a light as possible. To hear Coffee's version, Baines led them to the wagons with the purest of intentions, only to be attacked by a bunch of ten or so Texans for no reason. One important omission to the story was the desertion of Brown. During the ride to the Whangdoodle, Coffee and the men decided it might be best for all concerned if they kept secret that fact that they left a wounded man behind.

While guessing that Coffee lied, Donglar did not force the issue. Baines had been a useful man, possessing many good contacts—and numerous faults. However, the gunman had served his purpose and become an expensive luxury. Word would be spreading over the prairie telegraph that men with guns could find employment at the Whangdoodle, Baines had seen to that. So his death meant no more to Donglar than a saving of money.

"Take the men to the bunkhouse, Coffee," he said.

Studying Donglar's frilly-bosomed shirt, town style trousers and shoes, a stocky, scar-faced man made no attempt to follow Coffee's lead at departure.

"Just one thing, mister," the scarred man said. "We haven't talked about why we're here—or about money."

All the men halted, turning their attention first to the speaker, then in Donglar's direction. Throwing a startled look at the two men, Coffee opened his mouth, but Donglar beat him to it.

"You're here to take orders. Like Baines told you, the pay will be between fifty and seventy-five and found."

"That's what Baines said, Scar," Coffee put in.

Ignoring Coffee, Scar still faced Donglar. "Just what orders do we take?"

"Any I choose to give."

Slowly the scarred man dropped his eyes to re-study the most important item of Donglar's dress. Around the handsome man's waist hung a gunbelt, although not of the normal type seen in the West. It rode high and the holster, though well-made and fitting the Merwin and Hulbert Army Pocket revolver correctly, slanted its tip to the rear in a manner which struck Scar as being awkward and impractical. No man could possibly make a fast draw from such a rig, Scar concluded; and he had a rooted objection to taking orders from a dude.

"And who're——" he began.

"Choke off, Scar!" Coffee put it urgently. "The boys're tired and hungry, Mr. Jarrod."

Answering to one of the many names he used, Donglar

nodded. "That's the bunkhouse on the left. Put up your horses in the corral, you men. Coffee, on the way there call in and tell the cook to throw up a meal. And remember, all of you, don't talk about anything, or *anybody* you see around the place when you're in Backsight."

"We'll mind it," Coffee replied, throwing a warning glance at Scar. "Let's go, boys."

After directing another scowling, defiant look at Donglar, Scar turned and slouched off after the rest of his party. Catching up with Coffee, he jerked a thumb over his shoulder.

"You mean *we* take orders from that fancy-dressed dude?"

"Scar," said Coffee sadly. "You ain't pretty, you ain't clean, but try to show the sense of a seam squirrel. Happen you sell him short, you won't live long enough to learn how wrong you were."

While speaking, Coffee wondered if he ought to have mentioned his suspicions as to the identity of the man whose lightning fast reactions brought about Baines's death. He decided to leave things lie. Various factors pointed to Donglar's wanting Dusty Fog dead and Coffee felt that his employer might take exception to hearing that the six men had been so close to the Rio Hondo gun-wizard without attempting to earn the reward poster's bounty.

Donglar watched the men depart and a frown creased his brow. That mean, scar-faced cuss might need a lesson in manners, probably would. However, the lesson could wait until a larger audience gathered to benefit by it. A faint shudder ran through him as he turned towards the house. Going inside would certainly entail him in another show of affection from Anthea and he felt that he could stand no more that day.

Salvation, of a sort, came with the sound of approaching hooves. Donglar looked in the direction of the sound and saw Myra riding towards him along the town trail. With both girls on the premises he could count himself comparatively safe from either's passions; but it was like walking about a gun-powder store tossing lit matches at the barrels.

Riding directly to the stables on the left of the building, Myra waved in a beckoning manner to Donglar. He thought of ignoring the gesture, but she repeated it with an angry, imperious movement. Rather than chance a scene in plain view of the house, Donglar walked towards the stables and Myra entered the building.

Two arms flung themselves around Donglar's neck the moment he passed through the doors and a hot, hungry mouth crushed against his. Only by accepting and returning the kiss did Donglar manage to escape from Myra's arms.

"What did you learn in town?" he asked, holding her at arm's length.

"That straw looks so soft and inviting," purred Myra.

At that moment nothing looked less soft and inviting to Donglar, especially taken with what lying on it entailed.

"Sure," he agreed, knowing better than express his thoughts. "But Anthea may have seen us come in."

"What difference does that make?" Myra spat out. "When we're married, it won't make a difference what she thinks. She's not my keeper—or yours."

"We need her," Donglar pointed out.

"Why do we? Both of us know enough about the plans to put them through."

"Only we don't know where she banks the money for carrying them out; and probably couldn't get it if we did."

"I still don't see why we have to pretend——"

"It's for the best, believe me," Donglar answered, speaking the truth for once. "There's nothing between Anthea and me. But she's been in jail for a long time, kept right away from men. So she thinks that she loves me—I've given her no encouragement—but riling her might spoil everything for us. Come on, let's go up to the house before she gets suspicious."

With that Donglar turned and left the building, escaping

before Myra could give him another show of her affections. Leaving her horse for one of the hands to off-saddle and deal with, Myra followed Donglar to the house. On arrival, she found her sister waiting in the hall.

"What happened in town?" Anthea asked.

"Let me get into the house first," Myra snapped and swept by her sister into the sitting-room where she flung herself petulantly into a chair.

Face showing anger, Anthea followed Myra and sat facing the girl, but neither spoke until Donglar joined them and was seated.

"Where're the men who went into town with you?" asked Anthea.

"In jail. On the way in I did what you suggested. They had a few drinks and started to show me how a real cow crew went to town. By the time I arrived, they were in jail. That dull-witted, slow clod of a marshal proved to be something of a surprise, sister dear."

"I never saw any sign of it while I was here last," Anthea cut in viciously. "But I'm not——"

"You reckon he's smart enough to make trouble?" Donglar put in hurriedly.

"Let's say he's efficient enough. And he won't take bribes."

"You didn't——" Anthea began.

"If you mean, did I walk in waving a handful of money and saying, 'Can I bribe you?' the answer is no. I handled everything with tact."

Anthea sniffed, but once again Donglar spoke up to prevent an open clash.

"What happened then?"

"I visited the local justice of the peace to bail the men out. Unfortunately one of the men had almost ridden him and his wife down as he galloped through town and the justice refused to release them until morning."

"So you accomplished nothing there, either," purred Anthea.

"Only to meet a number of the town's prominent females, including Mrs. Louise Ortega," hissed Myra with such concentrated fury that Donglar began offering up silent prayers for assistance. "I've a number of invitations to visit formally and issued a few myself."

"To come out here?" Anthea snapped.

"Of course. Where else would I give a house-warming party?"

"It'll be all right, Anthea," Donglar put in. "You'll have to stay in your room, but the servants won't talk."

Using his specialized knowledge, Donglar imported a staff of Chinese house servants. Only one of them spoke sufficient English to make conversation—although most of the others understood conventional orders—and he, as their leader and a member of one of the criminal tongs, could be relied upon to keep the rest in line.

"We'll have to get rid of the marshal," Myra stated.

"That's true," agreed her sister. "The essence of our plan to stir up bad trouble between the ranch crews and townsfolk depends on our men treeing the town. Once one ranch crew does it, the others will want to try. They always want to do better than their rivals. But if they know there's a marshal who won't stand any nonsense—and can back his play— they'll behave in town."

"We hire men who can handle him, don't we?" asked Myra.

"Baines can," agreed Anthea.

"Baines is dead," Donglar informed them. "I was told a pack of lies, but it comes down to how Baines's bunch saw a small wagon train and went in to help themselves. Only the men of the train fought back and Baines died."

"Will that affect our plans?" Anthea asked worriedly.

"He was good with a gun, but my man Edwards is as good. He'll be on his way here from Hammerlock with the equipment to reopen the Alamo," Donglar replied, then saw a perfect way out of his difficulties. "I know how to handle the marshal. The best way, and the safest."

"How?" asked both girls at the same moment.

"Randel is going to be shot, tonight."

"Do you plan to send one of the men after him, Charles?" Myra inquired.

"No. I aim to handle it myself. Shooting a lawman, even a small-town hick marshal, is a serious business. While our men might chance it, we don't want any of them in the position to be able to hold it over our heads."

"That's true enough," purred Anthea.

"So I'll leave now. Ride to Backsight and be there after dark. When Randel makes the rounds, I'll deal with him. Then I'll get my horse, make a circle around to the Hammerlock trail and follow it until I meet Edwards. I'll come in with him, present myself at the bank with proof of my identity as the new owner of the Alamo. That way nobody will suspect that I've been in Backsight before."

While neither girl wanted to see Donglar leave, they knew that their plans called for him to be in town and running the Alamo Saloon. The deal to purchase the saloon had been carried out, by mail, through the bank and without Donglar entering Backsight. Once established, the Alamo could become a spawning-ground for cowhand trouble—but not while Biscuits Randel kept a tight hold of the law's reins. Removing the marshal as Donglar suggested offered the best and safest answer to the problem.

"I'll be able to see you in town," Myra was tactless enough to remark.

"That wouldn't be advisable," Donglar put in hurriedly, before Anthea could speak and directing a confidential glance at her. Then he twisted his head the younger sister's way and favoured her with a knowing wink that Anthea failed to see. "We have to prevent people in town from guessing that we're acquainted. Out here, a 'good' woman—and you'll be in that classification Myra—doesn't associate with people like me."

"In fact it would be better if you gave the impression

that you completely disapproved of Charles," Anthea put in. "We can't have people thinking you know each other, can we?"

"Of course we can't," answered Myra with such complete agreement that Anthea threw her a cold, searching glance.

Much to his relief, the two sisters declined to give each other any opportunity to see Donglar alone while he packed his belongings. Never had he expected to find himself running away from such a situation, in fact, he had often dreamed of finding himself in a position where more than one woman eagerly sought his attentions. Like many another man, he had discovered that realising a dream often turned its pleasantness into a nightmare.

Not until some time after Donglar's departure did the sisters meet again. They watched him ride away and then went to their rooms. Supper brought them together in the dining-room and Myra remembered an item of news gathered in town—one which might have changed Donglar's plans had he heard it.

"The Ortega woman told me that Dusty Fog is coming here," she said.

The gravity of the words did not strike Anthea. "Is he?" she said. "That's fortunate for us. I thought that it would be weeks, or months, before those wanted posters set men looking for him. Now he'll be here and I can arrange for his death myself."

CHAPTER SEVEN

I Didn't Trust You Either

Whoever designed the lay-out of Pasear Hennessey's western establishment possessed a firm understanding of the special needs of its clientele. Standing in the center of a wide valley, it offered shelter from the elements, comfort after a long, hard ride—and stood a mere quarter of a mile from the international border's line. While a man enjoyed the varied pleasures of Hennessey's hospitality, he could be sure that on the roof above stood a look-out specially selected for alertness, reliability and fabulous eye-sight, alternately watching to north, east and west; the southerly direction offered no danger. Once a look-out had been caught asleep at his post and what Pasear Hennessey, the genial host, did to that man ensured that none of his replacements repeated the lapse.

Although he knew that the look-out watched him, Waco made no attempt to turn back, hide or evade the scrutiny. Instead he rode the powerful buckskin, one of his relay, towards the long, one-floor adobe building and directed numerous glances towards his back-trail in a manner the look-out regarded as being completely normal and natural in a prospective customer. Reaching the front of the building, Waco swung from his horse and left it secured to the

hitching rail along with several other fine-looking mounts
already tied there. A frown creased his face as he stepped
on to the porch and saw one of the wanted posters bearing
Dusty's name fastened alongside the doors. Remembering
his orders, he made no attempt to tear down the offending
document. Instead he thrust open the double batwing doors
and entered the big bar-room, acting in a manner calculated
to lull the occupants' suspicions.

The bar-room took up all the front half of the building
and for such an isolated spot contained a remarkable degree
of comfort. Of course the clientele, men on the run from
the law and headed to the safety of Mexico, invariably had
fair sums of money about their persons and Hennessey, a
shrewd businessman, gave them a chance to spend some of
their wealth. Several hard-eyed, gun-hung men sat scattered
about the room, eating, drinking, being entertained by Hennessey's female staff or trying to beat the house's percentage
and win at the various gambling games. Facing the front
door across the width of the room was the bar, long and
shiny. Behind it stood a large, heavily-built man with bay-
rum slicked hair and a face which showed mixed Irish-
Spanish parentage. Turning from the serving hatch at which
he had been speaking to somebody in the kitchen, he gave
the newcomer as close a scrutiny as did the customers.
Pasear Hennessey's eyes narrowed as he recognised Waco
as a son of the Lone Star State. Then Hennessey relaxed.
While expecting a visit by a Texan, or group of Texans,
this current member of the species was not one of the expected.

Watching the cat-cautious manner in which Waco entered
the room, studied its occupants, then made his way to a
table near the doors and took a seat with his back to the
wall, Hennessey drew the conclusions the youngster intended he should. Since parting company with Dusty, Mark
and Doc, Waco had ridden hard, so he presented a significant gaunt, unwashed and unshaven appearance. Also, most

of his growing years had been spent among a certain class of men and he could mimic their manner and ways perfectly. Hennessey had not the slightest doubt, studying Waco, that the youngster was on the run and headed hurriedly for the safety of the border.

"Bring me a meal," Waco ordered, conscious of Hennessey's scrutiny, as a waiter came to the table.

"And *tequila, senor?*"

"Sure, but not until I've eaten."

Having satisfied himself that Waco was *persona grata,* Hennessey tried to decide whether the youngster would be worth cultivating. Among his other services, the saloon-keeper acted as an employment bureau—taking an impartial fee from both employer and work-seeker. He wondered which of his clients might like the services of such an obviously efficient young man. Of course, finding an employer depended on whether the young man could accept work in the United States or if his past infringements of the law meant that he must stay below the Mexican border for a time.

Before Hennessey could decide on how to approach the tricky business of gaining Waco's confidence, he found himself called to the door alongside the bar, and which led into the rear section of the building, to deal with some administration problem. By the time Hennessey found himself free again, Waco had finished the meal, and the drumming of approaching hooves heralded the arrival of another customer. Hennessey waited to see who the new arrival might be.

A tall young Texas man carrying an exceptionally fine Winchester rifle stepped into the room. For a moment Hennessey stared, then as recognition came he felt his nerves twang a nervous warning. Despite the grey shirt, blue jeans and lack of the sheathed bowie knife at the left side—and in the face of Hennessey's grim-given warnings to the look-out—the Ysabel Kid stood before the saloon-keeper, cold red-hazel eyes studying him sardonically.

"Howdy, Pasear," greeted the Kid, advancing some twenty feet into the centre of the room and facing the bar.

"Hola, Cabrito!" Hennessey answered in a louder voice than necessary. "I was not expecting you."

"No?" smiled the Kid, holding his rifle negligently in the right hand, thumb curled around the small of the butt, three fingers through the loading lever, forefinger on the delicately adjusted set-trigger, barrel slanting harmlessly at the floor. "Now me, I'd say you've been expecting me ever since you hung that poster on the wall outside."

Silence fell on the room, all activities churning to a halt as interest swung to the tall, Indian-dark young man. Possibly only Hennessey recognised the Kid in his change of clothing, but all had seen the reward poster and wondered if the new-comer might have arrived with proof of Dusty Fog's death and to collect the bounty.

"And what brought you here, *Cabrito?*" asked Hennessey, still speaking far louder than he needed if merely addressing the Kid.

"I want to know where a man can collect that bounty and who put it on."

"A man in my position cannot betray a confidence, *Cabrito.*"

"Reckon not," agreed the Kid mildly and, without giving a hint of what he aimed to do, brought up the rifle, its foregrip slapping into the palm of the waiting left hand, the barrel trained directly on the man behind the bar. "Just keep your hands where I can see them, Pasear, and then let's see why you keep on yelling my name."

A moment later in raising the rifle and the Kid would have died without a chance. Even as he finished giving out his warning, the Kid saw two shotguns come into view and line on him. The first inched its way through the serving hatch at Hennessey's left, although its user managed to keep well concealed. Gun number two crept into view through the crack of the door alongside the bar and added its twin-barrelled menace to the Kid's life.

"Don't shoot, either of you!" Hennessey spat out in rapid, urgent Spanish and cursed his rotten luck.

"Wouldn't be wise at all," drawled the Kid. "I'd still get you, Pasear, if they pulled down on me."

"I know," Hennessey said bitterly. "I've been expecting you to come ever since the first poster went out, and made arrangements. But that fool on the roof has——"

"Now don't you go blaming him. You likely told him just what to look for. Then I have to spoil things by going all sneaky and change my clothes, leave off my old Bowie knife and come up riding a sorrel instead of my old Blackie hoss. Wouldn't want to tell those two boys to put the scatters down, now would you?"

"I think now, *Cabrito*. All around are my friends and at any moment one or more of them will take a hand."

"Surely hope none of them's plumb foolish enough to try it," put in a quiet voice that came accompanied by the scraping of a thrust-back chair's legs and the sinister clicking sound of cocking Colts.

Turning to see where he had gone wrong, Hennessey gave a wry grin as he learned that for once his judgment of character had been at fault. Apparently the young man the saloon-keeper pegged as an on-the-run owlhoot was nothing of the kind. Waco stood up, a Colt in either hand, their persuasive muzzles sweeping the room with relaxed, but deadly, precision. At least, Hennessey mused, the guess that the blond youngster was better than fair with his guns had been correct.

"I didn't trust you either, Pasear," the Kid remarked.

"So it seems, *Cabrito*."

"Looks like the boy's spoiled your game. He can shoot good enough to take out both your boys."

"But not at the same time, *Cabrito*. Should he kill Pedro, Cosmos will still be there to get you."

"Only you'll be a heap too dead to enjoy it," the Kid pointed out.

"Possibly," admitted Hennessey. "Although I don't think much of your chances. One might call it a stand-off."

"Now me," drawled the Kid. "I'd say that all depends on which of us has the most to live for."

Nobody in the room moved or made a sound as the two main actors of the scene weighed up their chances. Everything pointed, as Hennessey said, to a stand-off. Hennessey knew the Kid to be fearless and capable of taking the desperate risks if only a slight opportunity presented itself. Not for a moment did the Kid doubt Hennessey's courage and willingness to grab any chance to break the deadlock.

"Well?" asked Hennessey at last.

"You wouldn't want to tell me who put out that dodger and save us all some fuss?" the Kid answered.

"No."

"Figured you'd go and say that. Go fasten open the doors, Waco. Then get our hosses ready and cover me with your rifle."

"Yo!" replied Waco and started moving crab-wise across the floor towards the doors. At no time did he lose his drop on the crowd.

"A cool young one, that, *Cabrito,*" Hennessey remarked. "He was not riding with you the last time we met."

"Which same's why I sent him here ahead of me. Figured you'd expect some of us to come calling once we got the word about the bounty on Dusty's scalp."

"And so I did. I thought the idea of the bounty foolish, but who am I to prevent a customer spending money?"

All the time he spoke, Hennessey stayed alert for any chance to break the stand-off in his favour. Yet so smoothly did Waco move, and so unwavering remained the Kid's rifle, that any attempt to do so would be certain death. Perhaps a chance might present itself when the youngster obeyed the Kid's order to open and fasten back the doors.

Realising the danger, Waco holstered his left-hand Colt on reaching the door, but kept the other gun ready for instant use. He drew open the right side of the doors, held it back against the wall with his knee and swung the retaining hook into place. Still without losing the drop, he crossed and repeated the procedure at the left side of the door. Backing out of the room, he unfastened the Kid's sorrel and turned it so it pointed away from the building. Next he led his own mount around so it stood sideways to the doors. Substituting his rifle for the Colt, he mounted fast. Before anybody in the room had time to make a hostile move, Waco sat his buckskin and lined the Winchester Centennial in the direction of the bar.

"I've got a right true bead on Mr. Hennessey, Lon," he announced. "You can do what you want to do now."

"Not going to tell me about that dodger then, Pasear?" asked the Kid, ignoring his companion for the moment.

"Not a chance," the saloon-keeper replied, secure in the knowledge that the affair stood at a deadlock; and also that his refusal to be bluffed into disclosing confidential information had a large, appreciative audience who would spread word of it among their class, bringing him much praise and extra business.

"You'll be sorry, you know that?"

"All things are with God, *amigo*."

"My old grandpappy always told me that *Ka-Dih* looked after his own," the Kid drawled. "I'm going now. Let's have no unpleasantness while I get the hell out of here."

Slowly and carefully, never relaxing his vigilance or allowing the Winchester to sag out of line on Hennessey, the Kid began to back across the room in the direction of the doors. His insistence on having both doors fastened back showed its wisdom as he moved. At no time did he interfere with Waco's line of fire or spoil the youngster's ability to cover the entire room.

"You want me to shoot, Senor Hennessey?" asked the

man at the serving hatch, suddenly aware that he had committed a *fau pax* in the matter of selecting his firing position.

"I'll tear your heart out if you do!" Heessy hissed back, without turning his head, for he knew he would be dead the instant his man pressed the trigger.

Then a faint gleam of hope came to Hennessey as he realised that the nearer the Kid went to the door, the more restricted became Waco's arc of fire. Unfortunately for the saloon-keeper, the Kid had also spotted the snag in the matter of his departure and knew that going through the doors would be the most dangerous part of the business.

All the time he moved towards the doors, the Kid watched the muzzles of the two shotguns follow him. He became aware that the man at the serving hatch had committed a blunder. From where he stood, the man, Cosmos by name, could not keep the Kid under his sights much longer without exposing himself or changing his position. Being born and raised in the Rio Grande country to the east, Cosmos knew much about the Ysabel Kid's reputation. One did not live to grow old if one took chances when dealing with *el Cabrito*. So Cosmos showed a marked reluctance to exposing himself in any way to the Kid. True a shotgun had great man-killing potential—but rumour had it that *el Cabrito* was no ordinary mortal and bore a charmed life. Cosmos did not doubt that the slightest wrong move would see him dead and the Kid escape.

Guessing at how Cosmos felt, the Kid continued to inch over towards where the man's weapon would no longer point at him. It seemed that *Ka-Dih,* the Great Spirit of the Comanches, looked with favor on his quarter-bred devotee for Cosmos refused to risk taking up a more suitable position if doing so meant exposing himself, even briefly, to the deadly accurate rifle in *Cabrito's* hands.

The second man, Pedro, realised what must have happened and, while sympathizing with Cosmos' motives, continued to keep the retreating Kid under his sights. Pure luck, rather than shrewd judgment, put Pedro in a position where he could aim at the doors without being seen or in danger from retaliatory lead and so he presented a serious menace to the Kid's well-being. Watching the Kid move towards the left side of the main doors, Pedro grinned. It seemed that *Cabrito* was losing his old caution for Pedro had out-thought him and knew just what the dark young *Tejano* intended to do. When the Kid made his move, Pedro would be all set to deal with it.

Five more steps, four, three, two, one, brought the Kid to the threshold and Pedro prepared to show his brilliant grasp of the situation. Finger commencing to squeeze the shotgun's trigger, Pedro saw the Kid make the start at leaving.

Only the Kid went to the right, not the left, hurling himself away in a move which seemed far faster after his slow, deliberate retreat. He went so swiftly that Pedro failed to react in time. True Pedro squeezed off a shot, but he had been so sure of his grasp of the situation that he failed to correct his aim. Nine buckshot balls, each .32 in calibre, slashed through the air towards where the Kid ought to have been, threw splinters from the door jamb, but did no damage to him. Taken by surprise, Cosmos failed to fire a shot as the Kid flashed across his line of fire and was gone from sight.

Vaulting the hitching rail, the Kid raced forward and made a leap-frog mount over the rump of the fiddle-footing sorrel and started it running. At the same moment, Waco let out a wild yell and applied his petmaker spurs to the buckskin's flanks. Already made restless by the shot, the horse sprang forward and carried the youngster out of danger from the guns at the rear of the room. Once clear of the door, Waco started to turn the horse so as to rejoin his departing *amigo*.

Up on the roof, the look-out had grabbed his rifle on hearing the sound of Pedro's shot. He saw the Kid burst into view and started to raise his rifle. Just as the man started to line on the Kid, he saw Waco appear off to one side. Unsure of which rider to take first, the look-out wavered between them. He hesitated a whole heap too long when dealing with a man like the Ysabel Kid.

Knowing the danger, the Kid prepared to handle it. Twisting in the racing sorrel's saddle, he threw up his Winchester. Even as the look-out wavered between his two targets, the deadly "One of a Thousand" rifle, specially selected by the Winchester Repeating Arms Company for its barrel's accuracy potential, cracked out. Firing from the back of a running horse was not conducive to accuracy, but it seemed that *Ka-Dih* still took an interest in the Kid's welfare. The bullet struck the Winchester in the look-out's hands, separating and rupturing the magazine, exploding its bullets and tumbling the metal-peppered man backwards.

With the menace handled, the Kid turned back and concentrated on keeping his horse running. Side by side, the two Texans raced along the valley until a bend in its length hid them from any sight of Pasear Hennessey's place.

CHAPTER EIGHT

Now It Starts Costing You Money

One of the few good things that could be said about Pasear Hennessey's general class of customers was that they minded their own business. Without a great deal of provocation not one of them would have thought of cutting in upon a private affair between their host and the departed Texans. So none of the men as much as offered to go to the windows in an attempt to see which way the Kid and Waco rode.

While big and bulky, Hennessey could move with fair speed, but by the time he had come from behind the bar, crossed the room and looked out of the windows, he could see nothing of the two young Texans. Giving a shrug, he went to the doors and unfastened them.

"I apologize for the disturbance, gentlemen," he announced, letting the doors swing together. "Drinks are on the house."

However, as he returned to the bar ready to distribute his largesse, a thought struck him. It seemed most unlike the *Cabrito* he remembered to give up a task so easily. Of course, the Kid was now an honest citizen and they did claim that made a man change his ways—but could any change be so complete? Most likely the Kid merely meant to go and collect reinforcements. Thinking of the nature of the Kid's friends, Hennessey, reached the conclusion that flight might be advisable. One of the reasons Hennessey maintained two establishments a good distance apart was to give him an alternative location in time of bad trouble. The business of the bounty placed on Dusty Fog's head struck Hennessey as about as bad trouble as he could become involved in.

"Cosmos, go up to the roof," he called as he went behind the bar. "Keep watch well, *Cabrito* may be back."

A few moments later the wounded look-out had been replaced and received medication in the kitchen and Hennessey busily served his customers. All the time he worked, the saloon-keeper gave thought to his escape. He had good horses in his corral and knew the country over which he must travel. Slipping across the border would not save him from the Texans, only speed of movement could.

After finishing his drink and listening to the hum of conversation at the bar, one of the customers set down his glass.

"Got me some miles to cover," he remarked and walked towards the doors.

Nobody paid any great attention to the man's departure at first. Reaching the doors, he shoved them open, stepped out—and returned a damned sight faster. Even as the man stepped through the doors, an unseen rifle cracked from the right side of the valley and its bullet sent splinters flying from the porch under his feet. Throwing himself back into the room, the man flattened against the wall and drew his gun.

Instantly every man in the room showed his concern. Not one of the customers could truthfully claim to be free from fear of the law's pursuit and all wanted to know the extent of the danger outside.

"Who was it?" asked a man darting to the side of the first to try leaving and peering through the window at the slope.

"I tell you something," came the reply. "I just didn't stay out there long enough to find out."

The question received an answer as a voice outside yelled, "Pasear. Hi, Pasear!"

Crossing the room, Hennessey halted alongside the window and scanned the slope without result. Not that he needed to locate the shooter to learn his identity. "Yes, *Cabrito?*" he replied.

"You going to tell me what I want to know?"

"Never!"

"Put it this way then. You're staying inside there until you do—all of you."

"Pedro!" Hennessey hissed across the room. "Tell Cosmos to get *Cabrito* while I keep him talking."

"Si, Senor," Pedro answered, without any hint that he thought Cosmos might succeed in following the order.

"Cabrito!" called Hennessey. "Suppose I, or one of my guests, want to leave here?"

"Just open the door and try," answered the Kid cheerfully.

"Damn it to hell!" spat out the man who had already tried to leave. "I've got a lot of miles to cover and that feller out there's got no quarrel with me." With that, he thrust open the doors and started to leave, shouting, "Hey, friend——"

Four shots, so fast that the shots almost blurred into a drum-roll of sound, the Kid's rifle fired. Once again bullets threw up splinters from the porch, creeping closer to the man's feet and causing him to make another hurried retreat.

"You warn't long gone," grunted a customer. "Looks like that feller aims to do what he said he would."

From his position on the roof Cosmos searched for some sign of the Kid. At first he saw nothing, then the reports of the rifle helped him pin-point where the dark youngster lay hidden. Cosmos had a problem for the rifle of the previous look-out was wrecked and his shotgun would not cover the hundred yards to the Kid's position. Just as he debated on what might be the best course of action, a bullet hit the inside of his protective barrier and screamed into the air with the vicious note of a ricochet. Its sound almost drowned out the deep bark of the shot, but Cosmos heard enough to tell him that the rifle's user was on the opposite slope to the Kid.

"Hey you!" yelled a voice from behind. "Get off that roof and stay off it."

"Was thinking that myself!" continued the Kid's voice and his rifle rolled out a further series of shots which tore chunks from Cosmos's position.

Grinning, Waco expended four shots from his heavy Centennial to further add to Cosmos's discomfort. The replacement look-out flattened himself on the floor and gave rapid thought to his position. Whatever his other faults, Cosmos was no fool and knew the two Texans did not miss him through bad marksmanship. He could not rise and deal with either of his attackers, for doing so exposed him to the other's rifle. With that unpalatable thought in mind, he concluded that the roof was not the place for him. Hurriedly raising the trap door, he slipped through its gap and down the ladder into the kitchen.

"Try that door to the left," suggested one of the customers to the man who wished to leave. The speaker also wanted to depart, but felt disinclined to make any rash experiments.

"Like hell," growled the other. "There's two of 'em and one's that side."

"What're you going to do about it, Hennessey?" growled another customer.

Ignoring the question, Hennessey looked once more from the window. He still did not know that Cosmos had vacated the look-out platform, although the shouted conversation told him that his man had been located. If he could keep the Kid talking for long enough, Cosmos ought to be able to locate and shoot at him.

"Cabrito!" the saloon-keeper yelled. "How long do you intend to continue this fooling?"

"You ready to talk yet?" answered the Kid.

Despite the "Why don't you do something?" looks thrown in his direction by the customers, Hennessey replied, "I've nothing to tell you."

"Then I'm stopping fooling. Now it starts costing you money. You've wasted enough of my time."

With that the Kid lined his rifle and began to methodically rake the front and right side of the building. After dislodging Cosmos, the Kid had taken time to feed a full magazine tube of bullets into the Winchester and sent ten of its fifteen rounds screaming down the slope. Both big front windows went in flying clouds of splintered glass; the side window disintegrated, its framework splitting. Inside the bar-room tables and chairs went flying as customers and employees took hurried leaps and dives for cover.

On the opposite slope Waco settled down comfortably in his selected hiding place. Close to his hand sat an open box with the gleaming brass heads of .45.75 bullets showing. He heard the Kid's words and the commencement of the bombardment. Studying the left side and rear of the building, he sighted his Centennial and cut loose with a couple of shots which punched holes in the side door. Then a fresh and more rewarding target caught his eye. From where he lay, Waco could see into the kitchen and recognised its potentiality. A pile of newly-washed plates standing on a table close to the window looked too good to be missed. Taking a careful aim, the youngster squeezed his rifle's trigger lovingly. Propelled by seventy-five grains of powder, three hundred and fifty grains of flat-nosed lead burst the window and the pile of plates erupted into flying fragments.

Having realised the danger to his valuable crockery, the more valuable due to their recent washing, the cook was in the process of advancing to collect them. Even as his hands reached out to remove temptation, Waco's bullet struck home. The cook, a short, excitable Italian, let out a screech of mingled shock, rage and pain as flying chips of pottery sprayed over him. Reeling backwards, he hit the hot stove with his rump, rebounded howling even louder and charged across the room. In passing, he caught up with his favorite cleaver, then tore open the rear door and rushed out of the building.

"Sounds all riled up," mused Waco, listening with admiration to the multi-lingual invective rising from the cleaver-brandishing little man. "Sure hope I can remember some of 'em to tell Mark."

Then, recalling his orders, the youngster changed his aim, sighted with care and touched off a shot which struck the blade of the cleaver and shattered it.

"Hi!" howled the cook. "W'at you doing? Don't you-a got nothing better to do than that?"

"You go tell your boss that we'll leave when he's talked," Waco answered and threw several shots around the cook, causing him to leap, dance and finally make a hurried retreat to the kitchen. After reloading, Waco emptied the magazine into the kitchen's windows and more wild vituperation rose from inside.

Rapidly feeding more bullets through the Winchester's loading slot, the Kid studied the situation and wondered how he might bring the matter more quickly to the boil. If possible he wanted to make Hennessey talk without killing or injuring anybody and needed a splitting wedge to open a gap in the other's resistance.

The horses at the hitching-rail fiddle-footed and strained at their reins, spooked by the splitting crack of passing bullets and sound of breaking glass. From inside the building came a wail of anxiety and a couple of men threw open the doors with the intention of securing their means of transport and escape from the law's pursuit. Working his rifle's lever in a blur of movement, the Kid drove the men back inside with close-passing lead. The sight brought an idea to him.

"I'm counting to ten, then I'll cut loose every hoss at the rail!" he yelled, rapidly replacing the expended bullets.

"Reckon he could do it, too," commented one of the customers, having watched the display of marksmanship from the side of one of the shattered windows.

"Yeah," agreed another and looked to where Hennessey leaned by the second window. "Hey, Pasear, that boy sounds and acts tolerable keen for you to tell him something."

"So?"

"So me 'n' the rest of these gents done took us a vote and decided unanimous that you goes out there and obliges us by telling him all you can."

While few of the customers had worked together in organized bands, they showed commendable co-operative action in the menacing manner with which they surrounded the saloon-keeper. Even Hennessey's normally loyal staff appeared to have turned against their leader. Led by the still-fuming cook, who now wielded a long and sharp butcher's knife, the employees descended on Hennessey and added their demands to those of the customers.

Giving a shrug, Hennessey looked around the crowd. "If you insist——"

"You can bet your life we insist," agreed the spokesman. "Now you go tell him what he wants to know."

However, the saloon-keeper knew better than walk out of the door without first taking an elementary precaution.

"Cabrito!" he yelled.

"I hear you and've got to nine."

"Then stop counting. I'm coming out."

"Thought you'd come round to seeing it my way," the Kid announced. "But happen there's any tricky games, I'll stop shooting to scare."

"You'd best believe him, gents," came Waco's voice. "I'm still watching the back and this side and I feel the same way Lon does."

Hennessey looked at the half-circle of grim faces around him, knew he had plenty of witnesses to attest to the fact that he was forced into giving information to the Kid and felt easier in his mind. Leaving the window, he went to the doors, thrust them open and walked out. Crossing the porch, he strode along the trail down which the Kid and Waco had ridden earlier.

Still riled at the delay caused by the Kid's actions, the man who had tried to leave let out a low curse and drew his gun. Looking out of the window, he growled, "Just wait until that damned Texan shows hisself."

"Put it away," warned another man. "So far nobody's been hurt. Which same wasn't 'cause that feller there can't shoot."

"And," another man went on, drawing and cocking his Colt, "seeing's how that young feller ain't promised not to shoot me, I don't aim to see him riled. So you just does as requested and leather it."

"Happen you gents feel so strong about it," said the would-be avenger, "I reckon I can forget and forgive." He paused, looked from the window and holstered his weapon. "Likely couldn't've hit him anyways. Ole Pasear's still walking and over a hundred yards off."

Alert and watchful though he moved, Hennessey saw no sign of the Kid as he walked along the trail.

"Far enough, Pasear," said a quiet voice from behind a rock which the saloon-keeper would have dismissed as too small to hide anything larger than a jack-rabbit. "And no tricks."

Only by exerting all his strength of will did Hennessey hold down the surprise he felt. "You've got a mean way with you, *Cabrito,*" he said. "Those windows cost money."

"All you had to do was talk," the Kid pointed out.

"I'd've been dead real quick if I'd talked. The man who put the bounty on Captain Fog's head's real fast, although you'd never think it."

"Who is he?" asked the Kid.

"Now there you have me, *Cabrito*. He didn't give me no name and I never got around to asking him for one."

"You wouldn't lie to an old friend, now would you, Pasear?"

"You know I would," admitted Hennessey calmly. "But not at a time like this. Why you've even turned my employees against me."

"Then I want what you know, Pasear. Happen I don't get it, you'll maybe need to build a new place comes morning."

"All I know is that he arranged to put out those reward posters and told me what to do. He left five hundred dollars with me and told me to hand it to any man who brought in those gold-mounted Colts Captain Fog won at the Cochise County Fair."

"The dodger said five thousand," growled the Kid.

"Somehow the man didn't seem to trust me with that much money," Hennessey replied. "Instead he said I was to tell whoever claimed the bounty to ride over to Dougal's place up Paradise way where he'd collect the rest."

"Reckon you've got the money on you."

"Of course. I wouldn't leave money lying about with those thieves I hire."

"Toss it over this way."

"And what do I tell the man, if he asks about it?"

"Unless you've changed a lot, he'll have a helluva chore finding you. Anyways, you've plenty of proof that you didn't have any choice but tell."

"There's that to it," admitted Hennessey. "Although he won't be the sort to listen to excuses."

"Then don't stay on and give him the chance to ask for them," the Kid growled. "One thing though, Pasear," he went on when the other tossed over a roll of money, "happen I find you've lied to me, I'll tell Pepper Alvarez who sold his brother to the *Guardia Rurale*."

A look of shock came to Hennessey's normally expressionless face. "Who told you that——"

"You just did," grinned the Kid. "Although I guessed, you and Pepper's brother were both sweet on the same gal. Pepper's not smart, but I reckon he'd listen to me."

"I told you the truth," Hennessey stated definitely.

"Bueno. There's only one other thing. Afore you pull out, start word moving that the bounty'll never be paid and that any man who tries to take it's going to die *real* painful."

"I'll see to it," the saloon-keeper promised. *"Vaya con Dios, Cabrito."*

Turning, Hennessey walked back towards his place. His stand against the Kid had been a gesture, a face-saver to prove to future employers that he could be relied upon. Nobody could blame him for yielding to the pressures placed upon him by the Kid's actions.

"What now?" asked Waco as he joined the Kid as the place where they had left the horses.

"We go and see a gent called Dougal."

The following night Hamish Dougal made his usual visit to the corral to make sure that everything was securely closed before going to bed. Running a ranch which served as a relay point for the Outlaw Trail, Dougal had little to fear from outlaws; and the local sheriff received certain additions to his salary which ensured that he offered no interference. So it came as something of a surprise to Dougal when a hand gripped his collar, slammed him into the corral's gate-post and held him against it. Cold steel touched his throat and he stood very still, trying to identify his attacker.

"I want some answers, *hombre,"* growled a voice mean-sounding as a Comanche Dog Soldier's. "Happen I don't get 'em, I'm going to whittle your head to a sharp point."

CHAPTER NINE

I Smell Trouble

Coming along Backsight's main street at noon, Mark Counter grinned at Dusty Fog and studied the deserted sidewalks. On the outskirts of the town, Doc Leroy held the remuda with the aid of a couple of youngsters from Caldwell's wagon train. Three men would have found difficulty in holding so many horses, so Dusty decided to accept Caldwell's offer that they travel along with the train. During the remainder of the trip, some of the youngsters travelling West helped handle the horses and learned many useful lessons in animal management. Reaching Backsight, the travellers halted their wagons pending a visit to the Land Office to learn where they might build their permanent homes. Doc knew that Dusty and Mark looked forward to meeting their friends in Backsight, so suggested that he hold the remuda while the other two rode into town.

"Let's wake them up a mite," Mark said, drawing his off-side Colt and aiming its nose into the air. Thumbing off three shots, he gave out a wild cowhand yell.

The doors of the Bismai Eating House, before which they sat, burst open and Maisie appeared, a double-barrelled ten-gauge shotgun in her hands. Anger showed on her face, but it died, to be replaced by relief as she recognised the two Texans.

"I always knew old Biscuits was lazy," grinned Dusty, "but I never figured he'd have you doing his law work for him, Maisie."

"Where is the fattest marshal west of the Pecos?" Mark went on.

"In the back," Maisie replied, the shotgun's barrels slanting down to the ground. "He was shot last night."

Pin-wheeling his Colt back into its holster, Mark dropped from the bloodbay and Dusty swung out of his paint's saddle.

"I'm sorry, Maisie," the blond giant stated.

"You couldn't have known," she answered.

"How'd it happen?" asked Dusty, getting to the point without waste of time. "And how bad is it?"

"It could have been worse, but it's pretty bad," Maisie answered, trying to keep any emotion from showing in her voice. "He's still unconscious, lost a lot of blood, so we don't know much about how it happened."

"Is the doctor with him?" Mark asked, thinking that maybe Doc Leroy's services might be needed.

"He just left. It's Doctor Wilmott who came out on the train with us."

"He's a good man," Dusty said.

"Where'd the shooting happen, Maisie?" Mark inquired.

"At the edge of town. Biscuits must have been making his late rounds when it happened. The man shot him from the side, bullet went through his arm at the right. Doc says that's what saved him."

Only by exerting all her will-power could Maisie keep the anxiety and concern she felt for her husband out of her voice. Yet she knew that every detail remembered might help in locating and identifying the man who shot Biscuits. During the trip West and the early days of the town, Dusty had shown considerable ability as a lawman and Maisie wanted him to take charge of investigating the shooting.

"He was shot last night?" Dusty asked.

"Shortly after midnight. Biscuits always made a round

of the town about that time. The reason we didn't find him until this morning is that he always sleeps at the office when there are prisoners in the cells. So I didn't think anything of it until he missed breakfast."

"Who're the prisoners?"

"Bunch of cowhands who tried to tree the town. Biscuits salted them away for the night after they caused trouble in the Arizona."

"Are they still there?"

"Yes. I thought of releasing them, but decided against it when I heard about Biscuits being shot. But they were in the cells all night and couldn't have done it."

"Likely not," Dusty said, wondering how he could offer to take over the investigation and if his intervention would be necessary.

At that point Maisie suddenly realised that they stood on the sidewalk yet, also noticed the absence of one member of the floating outfit.

"Come inside and take the weight off your feet," she ordered. "Where's Lon?"

"Handling something," Dusty explained and followed Maisie into the building.

Not until she had seated her guests and called up coffee and food would Maisie go into further details about the shooting.

"Could those yahoos Biscuits jailed have had a pard looking for evens?" asked Mark, looking around the room.

"There were only six of them in the bunch he arrested and they're all in the cells," Maisie replied. "Most of them are trouble-makers. They could have had a pard come in. But after he shot Biscuits, why didn't he turn the others free?"

"Maybe in liquor, got all brave and went looking for evens," Mark suggested. "Then got scared off when he realised what he'd done. Did Biscuits have any other enemies?"

"Every lawman makes a few, of course," Maisie replied.

"But I can't think of any who'd hate him that much."

"How about the Considine woman?" Dusty put in. "I heard she's escaped from the Territorial jail."

"So she has. Although I think her hate would have been more against you, or me. After all, it was me who shot her. She'd have no reason to go after Biscuits, even if she was around to do it."

"You know where she might be, Maisie?" Mark inquired.

"Pinkertons traced her to New York and on to a boat bound for Europe."

"Pinkertons!" Mark spat out.

"Don't sell them short," smiled Maisie. "I was one, you know."

"We try to forget that," grinned the blond giant, for no Southerner held the Pinkerton Detective Agency in high esteem.

"They are efficient though," Maisie insisted.

In this instance the Pinkerton Agency had been too efficient and followed a very clever false trail arranged by Donglar. The woman trailed across country, while resembling Anthea Considine—even down to wearing, and letting be seen, a leather cuff around her right arm—was no more than a saloon girl and now enjoyed a boat trip, being under orders to disappear in London, England, for a time.

"Who's handling the law in town?" Dusty asked casually.

A shade too casually, for Maisie felt relief at the words and saw one of her problems, how to suggest that he take over the office for a time, solved.

"Nobody, Biscuits never had a deputy. We never have any real need for it. The sheriff down at the county seat doesn't bother us much up here and Biscuits draws pay as his deputy."

Before any of the party could make more conversation, the main door opened and a trio of men entered. Coming to his feet, Dusty smiled and held out his hand to the approaching trio for he knew them all. Big, burly Jim Lourde, once a Confederate Army sergeant-major and now owner of a prosperous freighting outfit, took the small Texan's hand. Thad Cauldon, the local gunsmith, greeted the Texans and Doctor Wilmott showed some relief as he looked at two of the quartet of men who helped bring their wagon train safely to Backsight.

"Maisie told you, Cap'n?" asked Lourde.

"She told me," agreed Dusty.

"We've just held a meeting of the Civic Council, Maisie," Cauldon went on. "Biscuits will be paid fully as long as he's off his feet. But we'll have to get a temporary replacement."

"It'll be a couple of months at least before he's fully fit for duty," Wilmott warned. "And an unfit lawman's a danger to himself."

"Don't worry!" Marsie stated firmly. "Biscuits won't be back to duty until he's fully recovered."

"Which means he won't," grinned Lourde, then lost his smile. "We wondered if you could suggest anybody to replace Biscuits, Maisie?"

"Why not come on out and ask Dusty here?" she smiled.

"I can hold the town for a week or so, until you can bring in somebody," Dusty told the men without waiting to be asked. "Loan me a couple of men, Jim. I want the horses I've brought taken out to Colonel Raines's place. Doc Leroy'll go along with them. Mark and I're going to be busy for a spell."

"I'll attend to it," Lourde promised, knowing in what direction the Texans' activities would be directed. "Come down to the jail and we'll give you the oath of office."

Shortly after, Dusty and Mark stood in the office of the jail building and pinned on their badges. Without wasting time, after being officially appointed, the two Texans started to investigate Biscuit's shooting. Firstly they interviewed the six sullen hard-cases in the cells, bringing them into the office individually and questioning them thoroughly. Faced by a pair of obviously tough and competent lawmen, the Whangdoodle hands caused no trouble and each of them stated that he knew nothing of the shooting. Dusty believed them and, on learning that all their fines had been paid, gave them a quiet-spoken but grim warning about their future behavior in town and told them to go back to their outfit.

"I don't like it, Mark," Dusty said as they watched the Whangdoodle hands leave town in a far quieter manner than used on entrance. "Don't ask me why, but I smell trouble."

During the years he had ridden with Dusty, Mark could remember other times when his companion had the instinct for trouble—it always came shortly after.

"You reckon there's more than just revenge or an accident behind Biscuits being shot?" asked the blond giant.

"I don't know. All I know is, nobody shoots a lawman without damned good cause. Now all we have to do is learn why."

"Best take a look at where it happened," Mark suggested.

"Know something, Mark?" asked Dusty as they walked towards the place where Biscuits had been found. "I wish Lon was here."

"Which makes two of us," Mark agreed.

While both of them could do a certain amount of sign-reading, neither thought he could handle such a chore as well as the Kid. Maybe that Indian-dark young man could have found some sign left by Biscuits's assailant, but the hard-packed ground kept its secrets from Dusty and Mark.

"Let's make the rounds and start asking questions," Dusty said.

During the time they held law badges in Quiet Town and Mulrooney, Dusty and Mark had handled murder investigations and knew the routine. Despite their attempts, neither Texan could find anybody able to shed any light on the affair. Eddy Last stated that to the best of his knowledge no other Whangdoodle hands visited town, nor had any strangers been into his place the previous night. None of the people living close to the scene of the shooting could say for sure if they heard the shot. Visiting the livery barn, Dusty learned that no stranger had put up his horse. Mark saw Doctor Wilmott and obtained the bullet taken from Biscuits's big frame. While distorted, it appeared to be whole and might possibly tell the Texans something. With that thought in mind, Dusty and Mark made their way towards Cauldon's gunsmith shop.

So busy had the two Texans been that neither noticed the passing of time. On entering the shop, they found that their work had lasted long enough for Caldwell to have settled his business. The young man stood at the counter of the shop and held a Remington Double Derringer in his hands. Clearly Cauldon's business was doing well, for he had a good display of arms, ammunition, other shooting items and fishing tackle about the place.

"I thought, after what happened on the way here, that I'd buy a house gun, Captain Fog," Caldwell explained, although neither Texan saw anything strange in a man buying a firearm.

"They do say the time to buy a gun's *before* you have trouble," Mark said dryly. "How well can you shoot?"

"Well, I——" hesitated Caldwell, not wanting to admit his lack of knowledge to such competent performers.

"Have you ever used a gun before?" Dusty inquired.

"Not one of this type," Caldwell said evasively. "It's quite simple to handle though." While speaking, he proceeded to demonstrate his knowledge of firearms. "All one does is press the catch here, break open the gun," he performed the necessary actions, then reached for the box of bullets which he had purchased, thought better of it and merely went through the motions of placing a round into each of the super-posed barrels. "Then close it up——"

"And blow a hole in your belly," Dusty finished. "Do you have a sighting alley out back, Thad?"

"Sure thing, Captain," Cauldon agreed.

In common with many similar establishments, Cauldon offered his customers the opportunity of test-firing any weapon purchased. He led the way through the rear of the building and into a small dry wash. At about thirty yards range stood a back-stop made of two stout timber walls about twenty-four inches apart, the gap between packed with earth; not even one of the heavy calibre buffalo rifles could throw a bullet through first one wall, then the earth and finally out of the rear, so the range could be used without danger to anybody beyond the line of fire.

Taking the Double Derringer from Caldwell, Dusty broke it and, gripping the barrels in his left hand so that the muzzle pointed away from him, placed home two bullets. He took the butt of the weapon in his right hand and closed the working parts. The instant the breech clanged, a crack sounded, flame lanced from the Derringer's upper barrel and a bullet smacked into the back-stop.

"What the——?" gasped Caldwell. "The gun must be faulty."

"No. But your knowledge is," Dusty corrected. "The Remington Double Derringer's a fine little gun, but it has one real bad fault."

"What is it?" Caldwell asked, staring at the gun and remembering how he held its muzzle towards him when he demonstrated the wrong method to load it.

Opening the gun once more——it worked on much the same loading principle as a double barrel shotgun, the barrels hinging down from the butt and the bullets being fed directly into them——Dusty pointed to the striker of the hammer.

"See this, well with the hammer down, it sticks forward far enough to touch the rim of the bullet. Happen you try loading with the hammer down, the striker hits the rim and fires off the charge when you snap the gun closed."

"Then how do you do it?" Caldwell inquired.

"Just pull back the hammer to half cock," Dusty explained, demonstrating. "Now the striker's back out of the way. You can carry the gun safely like that and when you need it, just draw back and cut loose."

"Was it me," Mark put in. "I'd buy me a revolver, or a shotgun, they're a whole heap safer for a man who doesn't know sic 'em about guns."

"But I only want the gun to scare people," objected Caldwell.

"Then don't buy it," warned Dusty. "One thing you never want to do is point a gun at a man unless you're willing and ready to use it. Come on, let's see how you can shoot."

During the next hour or so Caldwell learned much about both practical gun handling and the deadly business of fighting with a firearm. While he had merely intended to buy the Derringer as a house defense to be used to frighten away intruders, he soon learned that such an idea was regarded by the Texans and Cauldon as stupid. Being a smart young man, Caldwell listened to what the others told him and accepted Mark's offer of instruction in the use of weapons.

"You'd best let Thad do that, Mark," Dusty remarked. "We'll have too much on for you to handle it properly."

"Will you, Thad?" asked Caldwell, looking at the tall, slim man and wondering why the Texans accepted the bespectacled gunsmith as their equal in such matters.

"I'll tend to it," Cauldon agreed. "Only you'd best leave the gun's purchase until after you know how to handle it."

"You couldn't be in better hands," Dusty told Caldwell as they left the building. "Thad's the best gunsmith in Arizona Territory."

Beyond that Dusty did not go, although he could have told Caldwell plenty about the man called Thad Cauldon.

After returning to his wagon, Caldwell saw his family settled for the night and then went to the Arizona State Saloon. His presence at the wagon would not be needed for a welcome committee of the town's ladies arrived to visit

and his wife found herself busy making new friends. In the
saloon, Caldwell was gathered in by several local men,
Cauldon among them. During the course of an enjoyable
evening, he learned much about the town and heard of the
wagon train which brought Cauldon and the others to Backsight. It seemed that the Texans who helped Caldwell also
did much to ensure the safe arrival of the previous train.
Caldwell heard of the various adventures run into by the
train, including an Apache attack which the Ysabel Kid
brought to an end by shooting the war leader of the Indians
at very long range, using a rifle borrowed from Cauldon.

Dusty and Mark looked in on the saloon for a short time,
then returned to the Bismai Eating House. Shortly after
leaving Caldwell and Cauldon, they had visited Maisie and
learned that Biscuits had recovered but was too weak to
talk. On reaching the Bismai, Maisie greeted them and one
of her Chinese waiters brought a meal for the Texans.

"I talked with Biscuits," she said. "He doesn't remember
a thing."

"We got the bullet weighed," Dusty told her. "It went
two hundred grains on Thad Ba—Cauldon's scales."

"Which same, a .45 Colt takes two hundred and fifty
grains of lead," Mark went on. "We figure a .44-40 Winchester bullet'd be about right."

"And that could explain why nobody heard the shot,"
Maisie said. "Whoever did the shooting must have stood a
fair way off—No, it was a dark night——"

"Sure," Dusty agreed.

"But up close a Winchester——" Maisie stopped as she
realised it was her husband she discussed.

"There're revolvers built to take the Winchester .44-40,"
Dusty pointed out. "We'll just have to look for one that
does, then find out where its owner was last night."

"It's as easy at that," said Mark. "I don't think."

"You never did," Maisie smiled. "What else do you
know, Dusty?"

"Not much," the small Texan admitted.

In addition to weighing the bullet, he had discussed the matter of the .44-40 caliber revolver with Cauldon and learned of one such weapon in Backsight. Although Dusty never seriously considered its owner a suspect, he still intended to check the matter until learning that he did not need. While Eddy Last owned a Merwin and Hulbert revolver chambered to take the Winchester bullet, he proved to have a perfect alibi. The previous night had been the occasion of a weekly poker game involving a number of prominent citizens and which always continued into the small hours of the morning. From midnight until half past four in the morning, Last never left the table. As the game was held in the saloon's bar-room, nobody could have taken the gun from under the counter and used it without being seen by the players.

"Which puts Eddy in the clear," Maisie said. "Not that I thought he shot Biscuits. Is there another gun in town that will take the .44-40?"

"Not that Thad knows," Mark answered. "And he supplies most of the ammunition used in the area."

"Who could have done it?" Maisie groaned.

"I don't know," Dusty replied. "But I sure as hell aim to find out."

CHAPTER TEN

You've A Chance To Earn That Bounty

"Looks like there're some more new folks in town," Mark remarked as he and Dusty rode along Backsight's main street shortly after noon on the day after their arrival. "Can't recollect seeing any of them with Caldwell's party."

"Or me," Dusty answered.

Early that morning Dusty and Mark had ridden out to the Raines ranch house where the small Texan attended to the business which brought him to Arizona. Leaving Doc Leroy to handle the remaining details, Dusty and Mark returned to Backsight for neither of them felt happy about leaving the town without a peace officer within its bounds.

Three wagons stood before the Alamo Saloon and the building's doors stood open, the shutters which covered the windows since its late owner departed had been removed. Several young women, clad in the colorful, bustle-rumped dresses their kind wore for travelling, stood by one wagon and some ten or more men worked at unloading another.

While approaching the saloon, Dusty studied the men. First he looked over the tall, handsome, well-dressed shape of Donglar and then examined the big, hard-looking man at his side. Both wore gambler's clothing, but the second man's were slightly cheaper quality and he had a good

gunbelt with a pearl-handled Civilian Model Peacemaker in
a fast-draw holster at his right side. A casual glance showed
no sign of Donglar being armed, but Dusty formed no judgment until he had had a chance to make a closer inspection.

"Can't say I reckon much to his choice of hired help,"
Mark stated as they rode by the saloon, having also picked
out Donglar as the boss of the party.

"Or me," Dusty answered. "Let's go collect our badges
and then tell him how things stand in town."

"Be best," agreed Mark.

The unloading had gone on during the time it took Dusty
and Mark to put their horses in the civic pound and collect
the badges they had not troubled to wear while visiting
Colonel Raines. Walking towards the Alamo, they saw the
nudges and looks directed their way by various members
of the saloon crowd. All work ended as the workers waited
to see how their new boss handled the local law. Setting
down a chair he had been about to take into the building,
one of the men, a bulky hard-case bartender who doubled
as a bouncer grinned and muttered something to his particular pards among the crowd.

Seeing two men—two obviously capable men—wearing
law badges came as a shock to Donglar, but he controlled
his emotions and his face held a welcoming smile as he
watched the Texans pass his wagons and step up on to the
sidewalk before him.

"Good afternoon, Marshal," he greeted. "My name is
Baxter and I'm the new owner of the Alamo."

"That'll please Eddy Last," Dusty replied.

"My business rival?"

"You might say that, although there was never much
rivalry between Eddy and the last owner. He and Eddy got
on real well together."

"Then I hope that we'll be just the same."

While speaking, Donglar looked both the Texans over
with the same interest they had shown in him. At first he

had felt puzzled at why Dusty and not Mark wore the marshal's badge. On close examination he saw beyond Dusty's lack of inches, felt the small Texan's latent strength and wondered who the other might be.

"You're fixing to run gambling in here, Mr. Baxter?" asked Dusty.

"Faro, chuck-a-luck, vingt-un and a few more things," agreed Donglar and nodded to the man at his side. "Mr. Edwards here's going to handle that end of the business."

"I'd like to look over the games before you start using them, Mr. Edwards," Dusty requested.

"Reckon it's any of your business what kind of games I run?" Edwards asked.

"It is while I'm wearing this badge."

"How long do you reckon you'll be wearing it?"

"Long enough, Mr. Edwards," Dusty said quietly.

"Unless maybe somebody takes it away from you," Edwards pointed out.

"I've yet to meet the man big enough to do it," Dusty warned."

"I didn't catch your name, Marshal," Donglar put in.

"Never threw it. But it's Dusty Fog."

Only a supreme effort prevented Donglar from showing the surprise he felt. A low rumble passed around the crowd and Donglar could read no sign of disbelief among his employees. Certainly Edwards did not doubt the small Texan's identity, for he seemed to have lost all his aggressive truculence and stood subdued, awaiting the next move in the game.

"I've heard of you," Donglar said, studying the man on whose head he placed a bounty of five thousand dollars. "But I didn't know that you lived here."

"Just holding down the marshal's office for a spell," Dusty replied. "And I'll be in to look over the games, Mr. Edwards. Let's go eat, Mark."

An air of tense expectancy rolled through the assembled

crowd as they took note of the town's geography with respect to the group on the sidewalk. As he turned, Dusty
found a further challenge to his authority awaiting him and
his way to the Bismai blocked. Tilting his chair on its hind
legs, back against the wall of the saloon and feet elevated
to the hitching-rail, the hard-case lounged at his ease. Between Dusty and the seated man, Geordie by name, one
burly, town-dressed rough-neck perched his rump on the
hitching-rail and a second leaned negligently against the
wall.

"You gents are blocking the sidewalk," Dusty pointed
out, almost mildly.

Without offering to move, Geordie turned his eyes to
look Dusty up and down, then dismissed the small Texan
with mocking indifference.

"I'm comfortable and there's plenty of room on the street."

A low snigger ran through the crowd, but Dusty did not
need its incentive to tell him what he must do. In a Western
town, a peace officer needed to keep the respect of the
citizens and he could not do that if he allowed people to
laugh at him. Unless Dusty showed straight off that he aimed
to stand no nonsense, he would receive nothing but trouble
from the Alamo staff; they looked that kind of folk. He
must teach Geordie, and the onlookers, a sharp lesson, one
which they would not soon forget.

"You've got until I reach you to move," Dusty warned.

"Happen you're figuring on shooting me if I don't,"
Geordie sneered, "I'd best tell you I don't wear a gun."

In so saying Geordie hoped to save himself. From what
he had heard, Dusty Fog would not throw down on an
unarmed man and Geordie figured he could take the small
Texan any other way, even without the backing of Preston
and Dink. So he remained seated, basking in the knowledge
that his boss gave tacit approval to his actions, and the warm
glow of being the center of attraction.

While Mark stood fast, Dusty advanced steadily towards

the still-seated Geordie. Even having seen Dusty in action on many occasions did not dull Mark's pleasure as he waited to see how his many-talented friend aimed to handle the current situation. Apart from moving slightly so he stood with his back to the saloon and in a position to prevent any interference from the people on the street. Mark made no attempt to assist the small Texan. Unseen by the blond giant, a big, burly man appeared at the saloon's doors, looked out and read the implications of the situation. Easing open the doors, the man prepared to lend assistance by keeping Mark out of the game.

Nearer and nearer Dusty came to where Geordie sat, passing between Preston on the hitching-rail and Dink by the wall as if they did not exist. Geordie remained in his seat, tense and ready, although relying on his companions to side him.

Suddenly Dusty stepped in, bent, caught hold of the rung between the chair's legs and heaved towards him. Too late Geordie tried to bring his legs off the rail. He gave a yell as the chair slid out from under him and went crashing to the hard boards of the sidewalk with a bone-jarring thud.

Seeing his friend's humiliation, Preston prepared to take revenge on the small Texan who laid Geordie low. Over a period of years, Preston and Dink had perfected a system for handling such a situation and they went into it without any need for discussion or thought. Thrusting himself from the hitching-rail, Preston raised his right foot ready to deliver a stamping forward-kick into Dusty's side; propelling the unexpecting victim into Dink's waiting arms.

Even as the opening moves were made by the main characters of the scene, the burly man lunged forward and enfolded Mark in a bear-like hug from the rear. He clamped his grip around Mark's arms, pinning them down with the intention of rendering the blond giant immobile and open to any treatment other members of the watching crowd might care to inflict. However none of the others moved, their attention remaining on the attack launched by Preston against Dusty. Not that the burly bouncer cared, figuring he could hold his fancy-dressed captive without any great straining of his milk.

Having known that Preston and Dink aimed to cut in, Dusty was alert and ready to counter their play. Good fortune had placed a mighty effective weapon in the small Texan's hands, one he felt more than compensated for the odds being against him. The chair had been cheaply-made and unsuited to such rough handling, so the separating rung parted company with the two legs under the pressure of Dusty's pull and Geordie's weight, remaining in Dusty's hands almost like the chosen instrument of providence. While hunting a wanted man, a Chicago detective-lieutenant visited the Rio Hondo and enlisted Dusty's aid.* In return for services rendered, Lieutenant Ballinger taught Dusty how to handle a police baton with devastating effect. The separating-rung was almost the same length and weight as the baton and offered possibilities that Dusty grasped instantly. Long experience had taught him the psychological effect— even though he had never heard the term—a dramatic handling of such a situation possessed. There were a number of ways in which Dusty could have dealt with Preston's attack and the small Texan elected to use the one he figured to be most spectacular.

Pivoting around even as Preston moved, Dusty took a short step to the rear. With the rung gripped at its ends between his hands, Dusty brought his arms up in a sweeping scoop that caught Preston's raised leg just on the ankle from underneath. Rising on his toes, Dusty heaved the caught leg upwards. Preston wailed as he lost his balance and pitched over backwards. In falling, his head struck the hitching-rail and he lost all interest in the affair.

The speed of Dusty's attack took Dink as much by sur-

*Told in *The Law of the Gun*.

prise as it had Preston. Never a quick thinker, Dink carried on with the prearranged plan by advancing ready to fell the victim as Preston's thrusting kick propelled him into range. Unfortunately Preston failed to do his part. Instead of being sent helplessly towards the waiting Dink, Dusty remained a free agent and capable of objecting to the other's future plans.

Twisting away from Preston, Dusty advanced and went under the blow Dink launched at his head. The small Texan's left hand released the rung and he thrust upwards with his right, driving the free end between Dink's legs. Sick agony knifed through Dink as he felt the rung's tip drive home. Even as the man reeled back, hands clawing at the place Dusty stabbed, the small Texan struck again. Around and across whipped the rung in the snapping, flick-of-the-wrist motion Ed Ballinger claimed to be more effective than a wilder swipe. Caught across the side of his jaw, Dink spun around, tripped over Geordie's feet and landed upon the other man preventing him from rising.

While Dusty held the center of the stage, Mark handled his assailant almost unnoticed; which was a pity as the blond giant gave out with a remarkably good display in his own right.

Actually what Mark did looked simple—until one considered the bulk and heft of the man holding him. Slowly Mark began to spread out his elbows from his sides. At first the bouncer could barely believe the evidence of his senses as he felt his grip broken and arms forced apart. Too late he became aware of the enormous muscles under Mark's costly shirt. Desperately the man tried to clamp down his hold once more, but felt the inexorable power forcing his arms further and further open. At that moment the bouncer knew how the man who caught the tiger by the tail felt when he realised he could not let go.

Then Mark stopped spreading his arms, stepped forward, turned and caught the amazed bouncer by the right wrist, gripping it between his two hands. Bracing his legs apart, Mark started to swing the bouncer around. Taken by surprise at Mark's terrific strength, the bouncer could not even make a token effort at defense. Such was the blond giant's power that he turned the bouncer and sent him crashing face first into the wall of the building. The impact caused the walls to vibrate and the bouncer stood for a moment, then slowly reeled backwards to collapse to the sidewalk.

After dealing with his man, Mark swung back to see if Dusty needed any assistance. A movement from the crowd on the street brought Mark's right hand Colt from leather and gave Donglar, who happened to be watching at that moment, an inkling of the blond giant's ability in that line.

Thrusting and rolling Preston aside, Geordie jerked himself into a sitting position. Humiliation and fury filled him as he thought of the way he had been handled. Not far from his right hand lay a means to avenge himself. He snarled a low curse and stabbed the hand towards Preston's holstered Colt, then froze before his fingers covered half the necessary distance.

Like a flash Dusty's left hand crossed and drew the right-side Colt, thumb-cocking it as the bore lined on Geordie's favorite belly. Never had any of the watching crowd seen such speed. Those who had secretly doubted the small Texan's claim to be Dusty Fog reversed their opinion and knew he spoke the truth. Donglar, having seen both Dusty and Mark produce a weapon, changed his mind. On seeing Mark, Donglar doubted if he would witness an improvement in speed—until he watched, or came as close to watching as possible—how Dusty fetched the bone-handled Colt from leather.

"Don't try it!" Dusty warned unnecessarily, for Geordie had lost any desire to draw the gun.

With the start of the trouble a small group of Backsight citizens made their appearance and converged on the scene. Donglar watched the locals gather and knew what he must do. If his men had succeeded in their intention of roughing up the two Texans, he would not have needed to worry what public opinion thought of him. Having seen his men go down in defeat, he knew he must make amends. Already the citizens scowled and muttered ominously, darting angry glances at the newcomers.

"That's enough, Geordie!" Donglar snapped, hoping to give the impression that his man could carry the affair further. Then he turned his attention to Dusty and continued: "There wasn't any need to be so rough, Marshal, the men were only funning with you."

Maybe there would be some of the crowd who disliked lawmen on principle and regard Dusty's actions as over zealous. If so, Donglar failed to locate them in his quick scrutiny of the local citizens' faces.

"Trouble being that I've a lousy sense of humor," Dusty answered. "They should have told me so—before they started."

"I suppose the boys thought that you was jumping a little too hard on us," Donglar said. "Some lawmen do tend to favor the old hands in the area."

"Likely," Dusty replied.

"I'll fire them all, if you want. It'll leave me shorthanded, but I don't want any fuss with your office."

"No need to do that," Dusty drawled. "Way I see it, any outfit coming into a new town's got the right to try out the local law—once."

"Just ask them not to make a habit of it," Mark continued. "Next time, somebody might get hurt."

"It won't happen again," Donglar promised.

"I reckon it won't," Dusty replied and tossed aside the chair rung, then holstered his Colt. "Let me know when you're set up Mr. Edwards, so's I can look over the games."

"I'll do that," Edwards agreed sullenly.

"Though you might," said Dusty. "Let's go and get that meal, Mark."

None of the saloon crowd made any attempt to interfere as the two Texans walked away. Watching Dusty and Mark depart, Donglar felt as if a cold hand touched him. While he had heard Anthea Considine talk about Dusty Fog, he discounted most of her stories about the Texan's brilliance. After seeing Dusty in action and talking with him, Donglar wondered if Anthea might not be right when she claimed the small Texan was the most dangerous man she had ever met.

"You've a chance to earn that bounty, Edwards," Donglar remarked, remembering certain boasts made by the other.

"Reckon I could get it done," Edwards answered.

"You'd better pick higher than that bunch," sniffed Donglar, indicating the sprawled-out hard-cases. "Get them inside and tend to them."

Then a thought struck Donglar. A part of the plan to make trouble around Backsight had already been commenced from the ranch. Maybe he should send word to the sisters to call a halt to their part until he removed the menace of the Texans. He decided to wait until after settling his affairs at the saloon. Some of the Whangdoodle crew might be into town that night and he could pass word by one of them rather than chance going out to the house himself.

"What do you make of them?" Mark asked as they walked towards the Bismai.

"Same as you. They're not the sort of hands you see in a small town saloon. If this was a trail-end or mining town, I'd know the kind of place to expect just by looking at them."

"And Baxter?"

"He's smooth; and dangerous. Could be one of those trouble-shooter house bosses some of the breweries and distilleries put in their places when they open up in a new town. You know, handle the local opposition."

Mark nodded. "I know what you mean. In that case, he'd

bring in a hard bunch to back him. What do you aim to do about them?"

"There's not much I can do," Dusty admitted. "I'll watch them, check their games are honest, make sure they give the local hands a fair deal." He looked at the darkening skies. "There's a storm brewing. Let's hope it's just the weather."

CHAPTER ELEVEN

There's Nothing Worse Than A Cow Thief

For three days the storm Dusty predicted swept across the Backsight ranges, alternating with driving rain and almost confining the entire district to its homes. So bad had the weather been, that it prevented Doc Leroy from riding into Backsight to join Dusty and Mark. When at last the rains ended, Doc offered his services to his host who needed every available hand to check on and attend to the storm damage.

Being new to the Backsight area, Doc rode with one of the local hands, a cheerful youngster called Flit. Although he had come West with the Raines wagon-train, Flit now knew a fair amount about cowhand work and was at home on the rolling Arizona range. Both Doc and Flit knew what to look for and the youngster possessed the necessary local knowledge to take them to the places where their services might be most needed.

The two cowhands made their way steadily towards the north-west in search of cattle which might have found themselves in difficulties after the storm. Knowing the area, Flit insisted that they would find the bulk of the stock in an area known as the bottoms, a sheltered spot ideally suited to offering protection from the elements.

"It's up on our line and where the Swinging L and Larsen's L over S come together," Flit explained. "I bet the bottoms are just crawling with cattle from all three spreads, and a few strayed over from Terry Ortega's place."

"That'll be where we start then," Doc answered. "Unless we find anything before we get there."

Which they did. On two occasions Doc and Flit had to halt in their passage and haul cattle out of mud-holes into which the animals strayed.

"If there's one thing I love more'n herding sheep," Flit stated as they rode away from the second belligerent animal rescued, "it's hauling cows out of sticky mud."

"They do say that good, healthy exercise keeps a man young," Doc replied.

"I'd rather be all old and ornery," sniffed Flit. "Thing I like about mud-hauling most is how them poor, dear lil cows run up to a man all full of gratitude at being saved. Why they get so plumb grateful that they're like to run all *over* you just to show it." Thinking of how he had been forced to make a flying mount over the rump of his horse to avoid the charge of the first cow rescued, he went on, "I tell you, Doc, them long-horns're the most ornery, cross-grained——"

"We started the breed down in Texas," Doc reminded Flit, overlooking that the Texans adopted the longhorned descendants of stock brought over by the early Spanish *Conquistadores*.

"Yeah," Flit sniffed. "Anybody can tell that. Mean as hell, all lean and too tough to eat, no use for the meat except maybe to shoe boots with. Them *Texas* longhorns ain't got a single good thing you can say about 'em."

"Horns make a pretty fair wall decoration," Doc pointed out.

In addition to their many bad points, the longhorn cattle possessed one virtue. They could live off the country with the ease of wild animals and did not need the constant supervision more docile and edible breeds demanded. When storms raged, be it slashing south country rain or raging north range snow, the longhorn would survive given anything like a reasonable chance of finding cover; although the longhorn could sometimes show a lack of wisdom in selecting a spot to wait out a storm. At one place Doc and Flit found that a small bunch of rain-blinded cattle had strayed into a dry-wash which became a raging stream of rushing muddy water. Following along the edge of the wash, the cowhands saw bodies lying in the mud along its bottom.

"Could be worse," Doc remarked as they rode away.

"It's bad enough though," Flit answered.

After covering another two miles, they met up with a pair of riders from Major Leyland's Swinging L ranch who were also on their way to the bottoms.

"This's Jervis and Sid," Flit introduced, indicating first the medium-sized middle-aged man then the taller youngster. "They can't help not riding for the best spread in the county. Meet Doc Leroy, boys."

"Never thought I'd see you riding for an outfit like the Bradded R, Doc," Jervis commented, extending his hand.

"Somebody has to show them how it's done," Doc explained.

While continuing their ride towards the bottoms, Doc studied his companions and listened to the flow of banter among them. Every cowhand worth his salt felt pride and loyalty to his outfit, being ready, willing and able to uphold his claim that it was the best at everything. Under the flow of abuse Doc detected a friendly rivalry but nothing more. The friendly atmosphere continued until the quartet came into sight of the bottoms, a valley with sloping, wooded slopes which acted as a rain-brake. Due to its winding course, the bottoms offered shelter from the worst of the storm and numbers of cattle appeared to have taken advantage of it. Before the riders could go into the bottoms, they saw two more men approaching.

"Adcock and Mitch from Larsen's," Flit remarked.

"They do say you can meet up with such nice folks in this sort of country," Jervis said dryly.

"They say wrong," grunted Sid, then lifted a hand in a welcome greeting. "Howdy, Mitch."

Studying the reactions to the approaching pair, Doc concluded that it was not Mitch who caused the comments and change in friendly atmosphere. Turning his eyes from the slim youngster, Doc gave Adcock his attention. Tall, burly, sullen-faced, Adcock struck Doc as being a typical bunk-house bully, Adock wore dandy, if cheap, clothes and sported a lowhanging Colt from which his hand rarely strayed; this combined with an air of truculence intended to make folks look on him as an all-fired hard-case.

"All right, Mitch," Adcock said, ignoring the others. "Let's go down and chase the culls from among our stuff."

"There's too much for us to handle," Mitch replied. "And most of it'll belong to Swinging L and Bradded R."

"Sure. You bunch'd better come cut your'n out and get it off our land."

Doc sensed the hostility around him at the words. No fences separated the different ranches, and their cattle roamed at will. For maintenance purposes the ranch owners adopted arbitrary boundaries, mostly following some natural line such as a river or hill range, but nothing prevented the cattle from one ranch crossing on to another. From what Flit had told on the way out, the bottoms tended to be in the nature of a no-man's land on the borders of all three spreads and so ideal as a storm protection zone that none of the owners claimed it. Adcock's words struck a sour note in assuming that the bottoms lay on L over S property.

Another possible cause of trouble sprang to Doc's mind, one which might take on serious proportions in view of Adcock's statement. No matter how thoroughly a round-up crew worked at clearing a range, some cattle always slipped the net and avoided the ownership-marking burn of a brand-

ing iron. Being gregarious creatures by nature, the unbranded animals soon rejoined others of their kind; but were
different in that the first man to catch them could apply his
ranch's mark and claim them for his own. Any loyal cowhand could be expected to brand any such unclaimed cattle
that he found. With three outfits present, the ownership of
the unbranded animals might cause dissension, especially
with a man like Adcock around.

"What'll we do with any unbranded stuff?" asked Doc.
"I reckon it's best we decide now."

"This's our land. They're ours," Adcock replied.

"I've never heard that the bottoms was on L over S,"
Flit stated.

"You wouldn't be calling me a liar, now would you,
boy?" growled Adcock. "'Cause I wouldn't like that if you
did."

"Way I heard it," Doc put in. "This's all open range."

"I don't see how you figure in this," Adcock answered,
rounding on Doc.

"I'm staying at the Bradded R. The name's Leroy, folks
call me Doc."

"You work for the Wedge?"

"I did once. Now I'm with O.D. Connected."

For a moment Adcock made no answer, but studied Doc
carefully and with considerable attention to the way he wore
his gun. Doc had on a short coat, its right side stitched back
to leave a clear way to his Colt and the gun hung just right
for a swift withdrawal. Pallid and studious-looking Doc
might be, but Adcock did not doubt his claim. The Wedge
had become famous for their ability to drive trail herds
through dangerous country, often with their gun-savvy to
cut a path, and the O.D. Connected acknowledged no su-
periors in salty, controlled toughness. From all the stories
passed around, Doc Leroy could stand up on his own feet
in both the tough outfits.

"What do you reckon we should do?" Adcock finally

inquired, trying to keep his voice hard.

"How'd you see it, Jervis?" Doc countered.

"Share 'em three ways and any over we chase off and good luck to the man who comes on 'em next," the elder Swinging L hand replied.

"I'll go along with it," Doc drawled. "How about you, Flit?"

"That's three of us voted 'yes,'" Flit replied.

"I'm making it four," Sid remarked.

"Can't say I agree," Adcock said.

"You, Mitch?" asked Doc.

While Mitch agreed with the majority, he had to share the bunkhouse with Adcock and knew the other's way with folks who riled him. So Mitch cast his vote along with his fellow-worker.

"That's four for it, two against," Doc declared. "Majority rules in this great democratic land of ours."

"Arizona's Republican," Adcock pointed out.

"We *all* try to forget that," Doc answered. "Even shares and all that we can't split three ways get scattered back into the wild country. Let's go."

Adcock opened his mouth to say something, then closed it again as he saw the others put up a solid front against him. Given a rough-house fist fight, he could take any of the quartet individually, but on so important a matter fists would not be the answer.

Swinging along the upper rim of the bottoms for some distance, the men finally turned and rode down to form a line across the valley. At a signal from Doc, they rode forward and started to ease the cattle ahead of them. Skilled riding kept the cattle moving and frustrated attempts to cut back through the timber. Towards midday the six riders had pushed all the cattle—except the inevitable few which slipped back and escaped—out of the bottoms and on to open land. The men decided to rest their horses before beginning the task of cutting their own stuff out of the gather.

After an hour's rest, Doc and the others resaddled their horses and went to work. For a time nothing happened, other than the decrease of the main gather and growing of four separate groups of cattle. Adcock and Doc worked among the main gather, selecting animals and hazing them towards the group which held the brand the particular creature bore. All stock carrying non-local brands, or without brands, went into the fourth bunch.

Suddenly Adcock jerked free his rope and flipped it over a cow's head. He rode closer, glared at her brand, then turned and waved to Doc.

"Just come and look at this," he said and raised his voice. "Mitch, come on over here."

Something in the sound of Adcock's voice brought all the others riding towards him. A flush of anger reddened Adcock's cheeks as he pointed to the animal's side. The others followed the direction indicated and all recognised what they saw. Burned on the cow's flank was an L over S brand with a line through it and just in front a Swinging L indicating that Leyland's ranch lay claim to the animal.

"The L over S's been vented," Doc remarked, but he knew something to be wrong.

A vent line burned through a brand meant that the animal so treated had either been wrongly marked at a round-up or changed hands since—provided both parties involved agreed to having the vent applied.

"And it's been done recent," Adcock answered. "A damned sight after the brand was put on."

Clearly the L over S had been applied at an earlier date than the vent brand, its scar-tissue showed that.

"Likely," Doc admitted.

"Anybody can see it has!" Adcock spat out. "There's nothing worse'n a cow thief."

"Just what're you meaning?" Jervis asked, moving his horse forward.

"Only what it looks like," Adcock replied. "We sure as

hell didn't change that brand, no stranger'd profit by doing it neither—and your spread has that Army contract."

"That's still sticking in your craw, ain't it?" Jervis growled. "It's been running a burr down you L over S yahoos' hides ever since we got it. I hate to hear loser's music."

"And I hate a stinking cow thief!" Adcock snarled back.

"Hold it!" Doc ordered.

On the words, his right hand made a sight-defying flicker and the ivory-handled Colt appeared to meet it in mid-air, its cocking click bringing a halt to all hostile movement—and only just in time. Jervis and Sid had come together and were reaching for their guns. While Mitch disliked Adcock, he hated cow thieves and stood ready to back the other member of his ranch if such became the issue.

"Who's asking you to bill in?" Adcock demanded, staring at the gun Doc held.

"Figure this's between us and them," Jervis went on truculently, but without trying to reach his gun.

"If there's one thing I hate, it's digging lead out of fool bodies," Doc explained. "And as I'm here and the nearest regular doctor's in town, I know who'll get the chore happen you fools cut loose—so you keep them in leather where they do no harm."

"You siding——" Adcock began.

"I'm telling *all* of you there'll be no fuss," Doc interrupted. "Ride behind them and take their guns, Flit."

"Nobody takes my gun!" Adcock warned.

"You want to bet?" asked Flit, riding forward to obey Doc's orders.

Although primed to resist, at the last moment Adcock lacked the cold nerve to call Doc's bet. One look warned him that the slim Texan aimed to back any play to the hilt. During the days when Doc worked as deputy under Dusty Fog in Quiet Town, he learned certain rules and put one into practice at that moment. "Take the man out who's starting the trouble." Dusty always advised for dealing with such a situation and experience had taught Doc that the Rio Hondo gun-wizard gave sound counsel. Adcock showed signs of being the biggest single cause of trouble and so Doc made him the prime target.

Acting as if he had been trained for such work, Flit cut in behind Adcock and removed the man's Colt. Still keeping out of Doc's line of fire, the Bradded R hand completed the disarming of the remaining trio and returned to the Texan's side with four guns in his hand.

"What's next, Doc?" the youngster asked.

"We'll cut the remainder of the gather and see if there are any more vented critters among them," Doc replied, then turned his attention to the others. "The first man to make trouble gets shot."

"And leave us not forget that ole Doc here's the only one present as knows how to dib out a bullet after he's put it in," Flit continued cheerfully. "So anybody he shoots is in one hell of a fix."

Throwing hostile glares at each other, the men obeyed Doc's order to start cutting the remainder of the gather. The cattle already separated were ignored as the riders went into action. Over a hundred and fifty head remained to be checked. With the discovery of each vent-branded animal Adcock grew more truculent and Mitch lost his easy geniality. One cow carrying the vent brand might have been overlooked, but not ten and more.

"Twenty-five!" Adcock hissed as they finished cutting the gather. "Not counting any that got pushed out without being shown."

"What's that mean?" Jervis barked, puzzled at the development but loyal enough to believe that his spread could not be in the wrong. He also disliked the implied slur on his personal integrity.

"Drop it!" Doc ordered. "This whole damned affair doesn't sit right by me."

"Cow thieves never have with me," Adcock answered.

"Sit still, Jervis!" Doc snapped, fingers spread over the butt of his Colt. Only in time did he give the order for Jervis reached down towards his rifle. "I don't know what the hell's going on here, but starting shooting won't answer it. Mitch, head for the L over S and tell your boss to come into town, Jervis, you ride in and pass world for Major Leyland to meet Larsen at the marshal's office. Flit, finish off here and tell Colonel Raines what's happened and that I've take the vented stuff into town with these two gents."

"I'll go tell the boss," Adcock said.

"I said Mitch," Doc replied. "You'll come to town with me."

Flit grinned as he saw the wisdom of Doc's decision. If Adcock went to the ranch, he might stir up the other hands. Mitch and Sid tended to be steadier, more easy-going and less likely to make trouble. The way Doc arranged things, Adcock and Jervis—the two most likely to start a fuss— would be separated.

"Why're we going to town?" Adcock asked.

"To let the law handle things," Doc explained.

"Law? Biscuits Randel don't——" began Adcock.

"Biscuits took lead and doesn't handle the law for a spell," Doc cut in. "There's a new man wearing the badge until he's on his feet again."

"You reckon he'll be any better at it than Biscuits?" asked Jervis coldly.

"I reckon he will," said Doc. "It's Dusty Fog."

CHAPTER TWELVE

He's Wearing A Merwin And Hulbert Gun

"Like to say one thing, Cap'n," announced the big, bulky, blond-haired Swede Larsen as he stood before the desk in the town marshal's office. "I know the Major here wouldn't have ordered that vent branding done."

"Thanks, Swede," Leyland, a tall, slim man who contrived to appear militarily smart and tidy even when wearing the mud-stained clothing of a working cowhand. "I don't know who did it, Captain Fog, but I'll back you in anything you do to find out."

Shortly after dark the two ranchers had ridden into town side by side and made their way straight to the jail building. They examined the vented stock, which occupied the civic pound, before returning to the office to talk things out.

"You'd best get the Kid out cutting for sign," Leyland suggested.

"I wish I could," Dusty answered. "Although the branding was done before the rains, so there won't be much chance of his finding any. But he's not joined up with me yet. By the way, have any hired guns approached you looking for work?"

"Hired guns?" repeated Larsen. "Why should they?"

"Maybe they thought there was a chance of fuss between

your two places. I heard there was some between you two over that Army contract the Major got."

"That was the luck of the game," Larsen answered. "I forgot to put in my bid. Mind you, the Major's hands and mine have been at each other over it."

"Just fist fights, nothing serious," Leyland went on. "My boys started crowing about the best spread getting the contract and Swede's crew objected. It's nothing more than cowhand rivalry."

"Why'd you ask about hired guns, Cap'n?" inquired Larsen.

"About ten or so have drifted into town today, coming singly or in pairs," Dusty explained. "They're sitting around in the Arizona and Alamo like they're waiting for something to happen and you know their kind, they can scent trouble like turkey buzzards finding a kill."

At that moment the door of the office opened and Larsen's foreman entered. "Boss," he said. "It's that damned fool Adcock."

"What's he done?" Larsen asked.

"Got himself a gutfull of brave-maker and talking up a storm about the Swinging L being cow thieves and how he's going to kill the first one he sees."

"I thought he was near on broke," Larsen growled. "Where'd he get enough to buy whiskey?"

"Not off me, or any of the other boys," the foreman replied. "Are there any of your boys in town, Major?"

"There's one," Dusty put in. "I told the hands Doc brought in to split up and stay away from each other. Where's Adcock at?"

"The Alamo, Cap'n."

"Reckon I'd best go down and quieten him," Larsen stated.

"You'd best leave me do it," Dusty answered, coming to his feet. "That's what the town pay me for."

"Watch him, Cap'n," warned the foreman. "Adcock's a

mean cuss when he's got the liquor on him."

"I'll watch," Dusty promised.

While walking towards the Alamo, Dusty wondered if he ought to turn out Mark and Doc. The two Texans were accepting an invitation from Biscuits and Maisie to eat with them at the Bismai and Dusty did not wish to spoil their meal. If bad trouble started, his two friends would be on hand quick enough to help him handle it. With that in mind, Dusty reached the batwing doors of the Alamo.

During the three days of rain, Donglar's staff worked hard to have the Alamo ready for opening. Only that morning a request that Dusty examine the games reached him. On checking, he could find nothing wrong with any of the gambling devices—a tribute to alterations performed by Edwards rather than the original purity of the equipment—and gave permission to use them. The saloon had been left almost intact, except for its stock and was ready for business. So far only a few customers used the big bar-room. They and all the staff watched Adcock who stood teetering on his heels in the center of the room.

"There's only one way to handle a cow thief!" he declared. "And I'm going down to the Arizona State, find me Mitch from the Swinging L and do it."

"I don't think Captain Fog would like that," Donglar warned, having seen Dusty outside and guessing what the words would do to the drunken cowhand.

"To hell with Cap'n Fog," Adcock answered. "I'd like to see him stop me."

At which point Dusty entered the room and halted just inside the doors. Although drunk, Adcock recognised the small Texan and saw a challenge which his whiskey-inflamed brain insisted that he meet.

"Get the hell out of my way!" he snarled and reached towards his hip—to find an empty holster for he had traded his gun to get enough money to buy drinks.

Having some knowledge of such matters, Donglar expected Dusty to draw and shoot the unarmed man down. If the small Texan had done so, it would have been his finish in Backsight. However, Dusty had seen the empty holster and knew the attempted draw held no threat against him.

Realization hit Adcock and he let out a roar of fury. Springing forward, he snatched a bottle from a table in passing and shattered it against the table's edge. Gripping the neck in his hands, he hurled himself towards the small Texan meaning to thrust the jagged edges into Dusty's face.

Watching in silence, the occupants of the bar-room waited to see how Dusty handled the menace. Probably all the crowd expected to see the small Texan's hands cross in that flickering blur of movement which brought his matched guns from leather with such deadly speed. In this they were to be disappointed, for Dusty knew of a better, less lethal way of ending the danger. Down in the Rio Hondo country, a small Oriental man worked as Ole Devil Hardin's personal servant. Popular opinion called Tommy Okasi Chinese, but he claimed birth in some place called Nippon. No matter what country provided his origin, Tommy knew certain strange fighting arts which he passed on to the smallest male member of the Hardin, Fog and Blaze clan; giving Dusty a method of unarmed defense that off-set his lack of inches.

Out lashed the broken bottle, its sharp-spiked points and razor-like edges aimed to lacerate flesh. Only it failed to strike home. Bending his legs and dropping his hips, Dusty sank below the line of Adcock's jab. Crossing his wrists, with the left in the lead, Dusty brought up his arms and, shifting his weight on to his rear-sliding right leg, brought his hands up under and behind the bottle. Dusty ducked his head in a circular motion which avoided the bottle, and transferred his weight forward to his left leg. Catching Adcock's thrusting wrist with his right hand, Dusty clenched his left fist. He advanced swiftly, closing with Adcock and whipped across his left arm. Instead of using his fist in the accepted occidental manner, Dusty swung it so its heel smashed like the head of a hammer full into the other's stomach. Just how effective the blow was showed in the way Adcock croaked, the breath rushing from his lungs, and nausea drove up through the whisky which filled his belly. Clutching his belly with the left hand, Adcock released the broken bottle from his right and dropped to his knees. Releasing the wrist, Dusty pivoted and struck once more. Again he did not use his hand in the conventional manner. Instead of clenching his fist, he held the fingers together and straight, the thumb alongside them. Like an axe biting into timber, the edge of Dusty's hand slashed at the back of Adcock's neck. The cowhand jerked forward, landing on his face as limp as a back-broken rabbit.

Knowing he need not worry about Adcock for a spell, Dusty swung around to face the occupants of the room. His eyes swept from face to face, studying the hired guns who sat here and there. Any one of them might have a wanted poster of the kind taken from the men who attacked Caldwell's wagons and could plan to make a try at collecting the reward. However, none of them moved, but all studied the fallen Adcock with puzzled eyes and wondered just how the hell it happened.

"Neatly done, Captain Fog," Donglar said in a loud voice and walked forward.

Dusty studied the man, noticing an addition to Donglar's clothing since the meeting and inspection that morning. A wide leather belt circled Donglar's middle and supported a gun holstered at his right side under the stylish cutaway coat. Looking down, Dusty noticed that the holster rode high and in an awkward fashion to eyes used to low-hanging Western rigs. His interest in the holster position died abruptly as he took in the bird's head crested handle of the revolver. Not the hand-fitting curve of the Colt, nor the distinctive shape of the Smith and Wesson. Only one model of gun Dusty knew had that style handle, with checked hard rubber grips and a lanyard hole in the crest of the butt frame.

"Where'd he get money for his drink?" Dusty asked, swinging his gaze to Donglar's face.

"My bartender took his gun as security for a loan."

"You let him do that?"

"Why not, Captain? Look, I'm new here and working in competition with an established house. So I have to build up the goodwill of the local hands. When that cowhand came in and had only enough for one drink, I thought I'd help him. Not wanting to give credit, I told the bartender to take Adcock's gun and give him a loan. It's lucky for Adcock that I did, you might've had to kill him."

"You could be right," Dusty grunted, knowing the other offered a logical excuse for making the loan.

"What about him?" asked Donglar.

"Take him down to the jail. His boss'll see him back to the spread when he can ride."

"I saw you looking at my gun," Donglar remarked, after telling two of his men to obey Dusty's order. He drew aside his coat to give Dusty a better view of the weapon and holster. "Edwards keeps telling me I wear it too high for a fast draw. What do you think?"

"It looks that way," Dusty admitted.

"I tried a Western rig, but it isn't comfortable for a man who spends most of his time sat down. Besides, I'm no hand with a gun and never need it. The only reason I wear it is because the customers tend to regard anybody who doesn't as something unusual."

"Man doesn't often go around without a gun," Dusty agreed. "At least, not out here. How about where you come from?"

"Back East? We've grown past the gun-toting stage there now."

"So they tell me. Well, I'd best go tend to Adcock."

With that Dusty turned and walked from the saloon. A wry grin creased Donglar's face as he watched the small Texan leave. It seemed that the plot to stir up trouble among the local ranchers had met a temporary set-back. Donglar wondered if he should suggest that the sisters suspend their operations until that soft-spoken, deadly efficient, smart man returned to his native Texas. Every instinct Donglar possessed warned him that a wrong move while dealing with Dusty Fog would prove fatal.

After leaving the Alamo, Dusty went first to the jail building where Larsen took charge of a groaning Adcock and promised to see the cowhand safely back to the ranch. Dusty walked along to the Bismai where he found his two friends seated in the kitchen and talking to Maisie.

"We're letting old Biscuits catch up on his sleep," Mark said. "How'd it go with Leyland and Larsen, Dusty?"

"There won't be a range war come out of the venting," Dusty answered. "I reckon somebody's going to be mighty disappointed."

"You think a range war is what somebody's trying to stir up, Dusty?" asked Maisie.

"Take it this way. Even if Leyland aimed to steal Larsen's stock, he's too smart to try anything like vent-branding. Since that cattle-stealing scandal over in New Mexico last year, the Army's been more careful about what they buy. They'd only take the vented stuff if it came with proof of ownership."

"Which means there'd be no profit in Leyland doing it. But Larsen might to lose Leyland the contract," Maisie remarked.

"He'd know that Leyland wouldn't chance taking vent-branded stock without proof of ownership," Dusty objected. "The only reason I can see for doing it is to stir up trouble between the two ranchers."

"But who would want to start a range war?" Maisie said.

"Somebody who wanted to buy land hereabouts," Dusty suggested. "Or somebody with a real mean grudge against this section—and mostly against Leyland."

"Why him?" asked Doc.

"This thing was rigged to look as if Leyland started the fuss. Folks would lay most of the blame on him should Backsight be in the middle of a range fuss."

"It'd take somebody with a real bad hate to start up a war that could rip this whole section apart," Mark pointed out. "A full scale shooting war could ruin a good half of the folks hereabouts."

"The Considine gal felt that way about Backsight," Dusty answered. "And Leyland was foreman of the jury that tried her."

"But she left the country after her escape," Maisie objected. "I had a letter from a cousin come in on the noon stage. I'll get it for you, Dusty."

Maisie's cousin proved to be an agent for the Pinkerton Detective Agency, and proud of his work. Reading the letter, Dusty found a detailed description of the Agency's hunt for the escaped prisoner. After reading the letter, Dusty returned it to Maisie who passed it to Mark.

"Well?" she asked, after all three Texans had read it.

"Did you notice anything, Mark, Doc?" Dusty said.

"Pinkertons seem to have trailed her until she left the country," Doc answered, conscious of the feeling that he had missed something important.

"They picked up her trail when some desk clerk in Santa Fe saw the leather cuff she wore around her arm," Mark commented. "Which same happened in Muncie, Kansas and again in Chicago and on the eastbound train. For a gal as smart as the Considine I remember, that's awful negligent."

"That's what I thought," Dusty agreed.

"Then you think it might not have been her that the Pinkerton's followed?"

"Could be, Doc," Dusty said. "Take it this way, Pinkertons have a reputation for being thorough. I might not like them or some of their methods, but I'll give them that. So when word gets out that Pinkertons have trailed Considine on to a boat that's leaving the country, other lawmen aren't going to bother hunting for her or the folks who helped her escape."

"That's true enough," Maisie replied. "Most lawmen have enough on their hands without chasing somebody who might not even be in the country. Then there were those wanted dodgers on you, Dusty. Considine had good reason to hate you."

"And you if it came to that," Mark pointed out. "Where do you reckon she is, Dusty?"

"This's a big country," Dusty answered. "Any ideas, Maisie?"

"Why pick on me?" she smiled. "Of course, I could say how about the Fernandez place. It has a new owner."

"Have you seen her?"

"No. She came in the day before Biscuits was shot, but I missed meeting her. From all I heard, she's well-bred and educated. Biscuits thinks he ought to recognise her and the description he gave me, apart from the hair, fitted Considine."

"Don't like asking the obvious, Maisie," Doc put in. "Could that gal be the Considine woman?"

"Biscuits and at least some of the women who met her would have recognised her. Anyways, she's a younger woman than Considine."

"I'd like to meet her," Dusty remarked quietly. "Running a lonely spread, with a bunch of hot-heads, gold-bricks and hard-cases for a crew's no game for a woman even if she'd been born in range country."

"Could ride out there," Mark suggested.

"We'll think on it," Dusty promised. "What do you make of Baxter, the new owner of the Alamo, Maisie?"

"Smooth, hard and dangerous," she replied. "He's been here for a few meals and always acts friendly enough."

"Ever see him go heeled?"

"I can't say that I have. Why?"

"He's wearing a Merwin and Hulbert gun."

None of the others spoke for a moment as they digested Dusty's announcement and remembered that its makers chambered the Merwin and Hulbert revolver to take only one size of bullet—.44.40.

"I know they never made it big like Colt or Smith and Wesson, Dusty," Doc finally said. "But there were a fair number Merwins sold."

"Sure," grunted Dusty noncommittally.

"Baxter's never been here, Dusty," Maisie went on. "I feel sure of that."

"He did come in with the saloon's wagons," Doc pointed out.

"But he didn't come all the way with them," Mark put in. "I helped one of the saloon girls across the street one night and bought her a meal here. We got to talking about Baxter. Seems that he joined up with them on the trail the day before they arrived. Come up from behind them and allowed to have followed them out from Hammerlock."

"Did you learn anything more about him?" asked Dusty.

"She didn't know anything more."

"It could be coincidence," Maisie pointed out.

"I don't like coincidences, even when they work for me," Dusty answered. "Why'd he settle here in Backsight? It's not the sort of town I'd say he'd go for."

"The town's growing."

"Sure, Maisie. Only not enough to warrant him bringing in an outfit like he has."

"If he's working for a brewery combine, he'd bring in good men to back him," Mark said. "And he'd bring in the kind of things cowhands like. Those big combines are willing to run at a loss for a spell to build up their trade."

"According to the bank, Baxter's the sole owner," Dusty remarked and grinned as his friends looked at him. "Sure, I asked. There's been something about him that riled me. Bank says that the whole thing was handled through a Prescott attorney's office about a month or so back. Baxter has stock from two or three different distilleries, which looks like he's on his own."

"There's money behind him then," Mark stated. "It'd cost plenty to set up a place and ride out the lean times until he gets enough trade to show a profit."

"Considine was rich," Maisie told him. "The law never laid hands on any of the money she stashed away."

"Say, what was the description of the man who helped her escape?" asked Dusty. "I only found the report of the escape in the office."

"I'm not sure, but I think that we never received anything other than that one short report," Maisie replied. "In fact, now I think about it, we didn't get the follow-up which the county sheriff promised us. Then when my cousin first wrote me and said Considine was out of the country, I guess we never bothered to write for the description. It didn't seem worth the trouble."

"You reckon he's in with her, Dusty?" asked Doc.

"I didn't say that, Doc. But if he should be, then a whole lot of things fall into place."

"Such as?" Doc inquired.

"Why Baxter brought such an outfit to a small town to open a saloon. Why he let Adcock get drunk and make war-talk in his place. No man who knows the saloon business as well as Baxter seems to would do that, especially in a newly-opened place. He'd know folks would remember it against him, folks he'd want to stay friendly with. Yet Baxter stood back and let Adcock make talk that, took with those vent-branded cows, could have stirred up real bad trouble."

"Which same a man who knows his business would know that a range war was the best way to wind up ruined," Mark continued. "So he should have shut Adcock up *pronto*. Only he didn't."

"Like Mark says," agreed Dusty. "He didn't."

"What do you aim to do about Baxter, Dusty?"

"There's nothing we can do without proof, Doc. But I aim to telegraph the prison at Yuma and ask for a description of Considine's helper. Let's hope the Warden down there's got a good memory and can tell us what we want to know."

CHAPTER THIRTEEN

The Men Can Have Her

Standing at the door of the barn, Anthea Considine watched a tall, blond young man wearing travel-dirty clothes and a gunbelt supporting match staghorn butted Colts as he rode towards the big corral. Idly she wondered what might have brought this stranger to the ranch.

For his part, although he slouched easily in his saddle, Waco missed nothing as he rode towards the headquarters of the Whangdoodle spread. The relay mount between his knees—his paint carried Clay Allison's C.A. brand which prevented him from using it—looked gaunt from hard travel and he had not shaved in days. Since leaving Pasear Hennessey's place, Waco and the Kid had ridden far and hard, following the trail of the man who placed the bounty on Dusty's head. While visiting an outlaw hang-out, they heard that gunhands were needed in Backsight and called off their hunt for the bounty-maker. The advice given to all would-be work-seekers was go to Backsight, hang around in a saloon and wait to be contacted. While riding to the town, Waco and the Kid discussed the situation. Using his local knowledge, the Kid failed to suggest one rancher who might be hiring. A chance meeting told them that Fernandez's place had a new owner and the Texans decided an inves-

tigation might prove informative. Waco elected to ride in
and the Kid would go on to Backsight to bring Dusty up to
date with developments. With the Kid's warnings of what
Dusty would do to him if he went and acted all foolish and
got himself killed still fresh in his ears, Waco came down
towards the buildings and examined the sight before him
with a calculating gaze.

Waco's range country instincts told him that he had stuck
pay-dirt. Nothing about the place before him looked right.
It was not the dilapidated condition of the big house, that
came from age most likely, but the general appearance of
the out-buildings and corrals. Dusty always claimed one
could tell the quality of a ranch by the condition of its
corrals. Most of a cowhand's work was done from the back
of a horse and good corrals meant that the ranch's remuda
received care and attention.

From the corrals, Waco turned his attention to the three
young men in cowhand dress who stood idly before the
house. One look told him their type and it fitted with his
views on the kind of spread he figured the Whangdoodle to
be. He knew the trio studied him and wondered if they took
him for a long-travelling hard-case looking for work—or
dismissed him as a youngster wanting to make folks think
he was one.

Apparently the trio tended towards the latter view. Billy
and Mick exchanged glances and it seemed that the lesson
learned in town had been forgotten by them as they grinned
at each other.

"Never seen him afore, have you, Billy?" Mick said.

"Nope," Billy agreed, throwing a glance to where he
knew Anthea stood watching. "And you won't be seeing
him much longer neither."

Since the fiasco in town, Billy had labored under a
sense of failure. Considering himself a ladies' man, he had
hoped to charm the boss with his personality but figured to
have lost any chance while in town. Maybe he could regain

the lost ground at the expense of the newcomer.

"This should be good," Mick informed the third cow-hand, watching Billy swagger towards Waco, and moved after his companion.

It was—although not in the way Mick meant.

Ignoring the trio, even when Billy started to approach him, Waco swung from his saddle by the horse trough. While his mount drank, he removed his bandana and dipped it into the water and in doing so turned his back to the approaching cowhand.

"Soon's he watered, get on him and ride out," Billy ordered. "We've no time for saddle-tramps h——"

Swinging around, Waco hurled the sopping-wet bandana full into Billy's face. Half-blinded, the youngster staggered back a few steps, hands clawing up in an attempt to remove the wet cloth from his face. Having followed Billy up, Mick and the third cowhand sprang forward with the intention of taking revenge.

Mick saw Waco's left hand driving at his face just an instant too late to avoid it. Hard knuckles caught Mick's nose, pulped it and changed his advance into a pain-filled, tear-blinded retreat. Seeing the power and precision of Waco's punch, the third member of the trio tried to halt his rush and draw his gun which proved to be a mighty foolish action, for the cowhand lacked the necessary training and ability to perform a fast draw during a hurried change of pace. Up drove Waco's right boot, catching the cowhand in the pit of the stomach and jack-knifing him over. Reaching out with his right hand, Waco laid hold of the cowhand's collar, heaved and shot him head-first into the waiting trough. Snarling out damp curses, Billy cleared his eyes and reached for the Colt in what he fondly imagined to be a real fast draw. Far faster moved Waco's left hand, dipping to bring the near-side Colt from leather. Up, across and out licked the Peacemaker, its five and a half inch barrel colliding with the side of Billy's jaw. Unlike its predecessors, the Colt

Peacemaker possessed a solid frame which made it—at close quarters—almost as handy a weapon empty as when loaded. So when the barrel chopped alongside Billy's jaw, it arrived with enough force to make him lose interest in the affair.

Even as Billy dropped in a limp heap to the ground, Mick let out a yell and made a move towards his gun. Waco brought his Colt into line, thumb-cocking it and conscious of a sick apprehension which came to Mick's face as the other realised that he had given a real proddy cuss a good excuse to kill him.

"That's enough!" snapped an authoritative female voice.

Waco felt a touch of relief at the words, for they gave him an excuse not to act as the kind of man he pretended to be would under the circumstances. Slowly, as if reluctant to stop, he swung his eyes from the rigid, terrified Mick and looked to where Anthea left the barn and walked towards him.

"I mostly kill any man who tries to throw down on me," he growled, not taking his gun out of line.

"Leather it!" Anthea barked back.

"You the boss's daughter?"

"I'm the boss."

"Do tell. I never afore worked for a woman."

"What does that mean?"

"Word has it you're hiring. You need good men, if them's your best. I need work, so there you have it."

Throwing a glance first to where the cowhand rolled spluttering from the horse trough then to the sprawled-out, moaning Billy, Anthea gave an annoyed sniff and turned to study Waco. Hiring the newcomer, even without having witnessed his ability as a fighting man, could be advantageous. Under the trail dirt and bristles lay a handsome face and a virile, powerful young body. With such a young man around, Myra might forget her infatuation for Charles and Charles was not the kind to be interested in a woman who did not stay true to him. So Anthea reached her decision and overlooked the matter of asking where Waco heard she was hiring hands.

"The pay's sixty a month and found," she said. "You take whatever orders I or my segundo give and ask no questions. And you never mention my being here when you're in town."

"Talking's never been my game, lady," Waco answered.

At that moment a rider came around the corner of the barn and approached them. At another time Waco might have found the newcomer an attractive sight. Small, petite, very pretty, with blond hair, and wearing a shirt waist, divided skirt and riding boots, the young woman sat her horse with easy grace. However Waco had an uneasy feeling that the newcomer's presence meant trouble for him.

"Good morning," the blonde greeted, her voice a cultured Southern drawl. At the words, Anthea started to turn towards the speaker. "I thought I'd ride over and—You!"

"Stop her!" Anthea screeched as the blonde, face showing surprise and a little fear, tried to swing her horse around.

Springing forward, Waco grabbed at the reins of the blonde's mount. Up went her left arm, the quirt she held lashing down at the young Texan. Seeing his chance to avoid capturing the girl, Waco jerked back and avoided the quirt's blow but what he saw and heard changed his mind.

"Help him, damn you!" Anthea yelled, bending with surprising speed and jerking the weakly-moving Billy's gun from leather.

Although Waco only saw this from the corner of his eye, his view told him that the woman knew how to handle a gun well enough to shoot down the newcomer. Mick charged by Waco, taking a slash from the quirt but grabbing and holding the reins. Jumping in, Waco caught the down-lashing arm and hauled the girl out of her saddle. Even then she tried to struggle, her legs lashing at him, fingers sending his hat flying and digging into his hair. Small she might be, but the newcomer had a fair amount of wildcat in her blood.

Gliding forward, Anthea swung up the revolver and struck at the blonde girl's head. Although Waco tried to swing the girl clear, the barrel of the Colt caught her hat's crown with enough force to momentarily stun her. Cold anger bit into the Texan, but even as he thought of drawing his guns and getting the girl clear, he heard hooves and saw another girl accompanied by three men riding up. Knowing that he could not handle that many, especially with the dazed girl slumped in his arms, Waco called off his plans until a more suitable moment.

"What's all this?" Myra snapped, bringing her horse to a halt by her sister.

"We have a visitor," Anthea answered. "Miss Louise Raines—or should I say Mrs. Ortega?"

Waco had already guessed at the blonde's identity and silently cursed the luck which brought Colonel Raines's daughter visiting at such an inopportune moment. Watching the sisters—or so he assumed from the family likeness—Waco formed an impression that no love was lost between them. He caught the veiled hostility in their voices, but drew no conclusions from it.

"And what do we do with her?" asked Myra coldly. "We can't let her go now that she's seen you."

"Take her to the house and lock her in one of the upstairs rooms. Later on the men can have her."

"Why not kill her now?"

"That would be too easy," Anthea purred, her face twisting into lines of hate. "I want her to suffer."

"All right, do it your way," Myra sniffed, then looked at Waco. "Who's he?"

"A new hand. After you've seen to these two, Mick, show him to the bunkhouse. Bring her this way, cowboy."

Waco hoped that he might be presented with a chance to let Louise escape before they reached the house, but did not find one. Still hampered by supporting the dazed, unresisting girl, he reached the main doors of the big house and Anthea led the way inside. A couple of Chinese in black clothing watched with expressionless eyes as the party entered, but Anthea ignored them. The presence of the servants halted the ideas Waco formed for rescuing Louise inside the house and beyond the sight of the hired guns. So he followed Anthea up the stairs, along a passage and to the door of a room.

"Put her inside," Anthea ordered. "Then you can go over to the bunkhouse and settle in. I may have something for you to do later."

"Sure," Waco replied and obeyed the order. He noticed that although Anthea secured the door, she did not take the key from the lock.

"Handsome young devil isn't he?" Anthea remarked casually to her sister as Waco walked away.

"Just another trail-dirty hard-case," Myra sniffed. "What do we do if some of her husband's men come looking for her?"

"You deny that she's ever been here. Only get rid of her horse and make sure it's hidden somewhere that it can't be found."

"I'll see to it."

Turning, Myra walked downstairs, crossed the hall and left the house. She collected her own and Louise's horse, mounted and led the other animal away from the ranch buildings. Finding a suitable hiding-place for the horse, securing it, returning to the ranch house and attending to her own animal took time. Almost two hours had passed before Myra joined her sister in the dining-room for a belated lunch.

"Did you do it?" Anthea asked as Myra sat at the table.

"Of course. Who was that new man?"

"I didn't ask his name yet, but he's tough and good with a gun."

"Did Charles send him out?"

"Of course. How else would he know where to come?"

Fortunately for Waco, the sisters accepted that he had been sent out from town by Donglar. Letting the matter drop, Myra ate her lunch and after the meal ended sat watching her sister take out, clean and load a Colt Peacemaker. A feeling of restlessness filled Myra and she wanted to go into town to visit Donglar. It had been several days since they last met and Myra felt a longing to be with him once more.

"There's no sign of anybody coming looking for her yet," Myra said, prowling to the windows and looking out across the range country.

"Why should there be yet?" Anthea answered. "They won't be expecting her back too soon. I doubt if they'll start worrying until after night-fall and then it will be too late to start an organized search. I think we'll leave her body beside the place where you've been branding some cattle."

"And leave one of the branded animals close by, so that they'll blame the men who did the branding for the killing," Myra agreed. "I'm not going back to the men. It might be as well if I went to town."

"Why?" asked Anthea, not liking the casual manner in which the other made the suggestion.

"Just to look around and see if there's any sign of trouble starting yet."

"You didn't vent many of Larsen's cattle before the rains. It's likely that none of them have been found."

"We did a fair number," Myra objected. "And I want to know if any have been found so that I can start the men changing Leyland's brand to Larsen's and making Leyland's hands think Larsen's men are doing it for revenge."

"You could start without wasting time," Anthea answered.

"It won't be as effective as if we do it after some of the vent-branded stock have been found."

Although Anthea had been the brains behind the scheme, she wanted to prevent her sister's visit to town and keep Myra away from Donglar. So she shook her head and said, "I don't see that it will be any different."

"Of course it will!" Myra snapped. "It will look too transparently a plot to set the two ranches at each other's throats if mis-branded stock from both of them start turning up at the same time."

"All right, go in," Anthea replied. "But keep away from Charles."

"Why?" bristled Myra.

"Because I told you to."

Myra's breath came out in a savage snort. "If I want to see him, I will. Anyway, he may have some news for us."

"Then he'll send it out by one of his men."

"I still intend to see him."

"You keep away from Charles!" Anthea shouted. "Do you hear me?"

"Don't tell me what to do!" Myra screeched. "I'm tired of you interfering and throwing yourself at him."

"Me!" Anthea hissed. "I've seen how you ogle him all the time."

"And why shouldn't I? When we're married——"

"Married?" Anthea interrupted savagely. "It's me that Charles is going to marry——"

"You?" howled Myra, almost white with rage. "The only reason he looked at you twice was to feed that infatuation and keep you sweet until we learned where you've stashed away our family's money."

Letting out a scream of fury, Anthea drew back and swung her left arm. She drove her clenched fist full into the side of the other girl's jaw, snapping Myra's head to one side and sending her sprawling across the room. Through the roaring pain and shock caused by the blow, Myra saw Anthea catch up the Peacemaker, thumb-cock it and line it in her direction. In that moment Myra knew raw fear. Hatred twisted her sister's face, and Myra knew that Anthea meant to kill her. So heated were the two girls that neither noticed a shot which sounded from outside at the rear of the building; even had they been normally engaged, shots were so common around the ranch that the sisters would not have thought the matter worth investigating.

Seeing the fear on Myra's face, Anthea did not squeeze the trigger immediately. Instead she kept the gun lined, savoring her sister's terror. A knock sounded at the room door, it opened and the number-one boy of the Chinese servants came in fast. If he felt surprised at the scene before him, he did not show it.

"New feller take the girl away with him!" the Chinese said excitedly.

Instantly Anthea's gun wavered and sagged down. Having been in prison, she did not wish to repeat the sensation and knew Louise's escape would mean just that unless stopped. Without a glance or word in Myra's direction, Anthea dashed from the room.

Myra lifted her hand, rubbed it across her throbbing mouth and looked down at the red smear of blood upon it. Slowly the fear ebbed away and rank anger took its place. Lurching to her feet, she crossed to the sidepiece and jerked open the top drawer. Inside was a Remington Double Derringer, serving the honorable and potentially useful purpose of house gun. Taking out the stubby handgun, Myra added a few of the bullets which shared the drawer with it to her armament. She dropped the bullets into the pocket of her skirt and followed her sister.

Tearing along the passage, Anthea threw open the main doors and rushed outside. Already men streamed from the bunkhouse.

"Get after them!" she screamed. "It's all our necks if they escape."

CHAPTER FOURTEEN

How Do I Know I Can Trust You?

Waco found Mick waiting when he left the house. Apparently the young man held no animosity for his ducking, but grinned amiably. Ever the opportunist, Mick realised that Billy's days as bunkhouse bully and top man of their set had ended, so he intended to ingratiate himself with the new leading light.

"What've they done with her?" he asked.

"Locked her up."

"What're they aiming to do with her?"

"Go ask them," grunted Waco.

"Not me. The old'n's got a mean temper and the young'n's not much better. Come on, I'll show you where to put your gear."

"I'll leave my hoss handy," Waco remarked as they went to the corral. "The boss gal wants me to handle something for her later."

"Hoss looks to have been rid hard," Mick commented.

"It eats work."

While he hated to neglect the horse in such a manner, Waco knew that he must at that time. Having his mount saddled and ready might mean the difference between life and death for himself and Louise Ortega later that day.

However, he did all he could to lessen the burden on the over-worked horse before heading to the bunkhouse with Mick.

None of the men at the bunkhouse showed any great interest in Waco's past life. One look at him warned the men who arrived with Myra that undue curiosity might not meet with the tall young Texan's approval and they figured he could make his point to any objections he raised. Billy and the other youngster scowled, but neither offered to take up the issue again.

Over a decent meal, Waco learned something of the work the men had been doing and, without being told, guessed at the reason behind the apparently senseless vent-brandings. He reckoned that, one way and another, he knew enough to end his visit and figured that the sooner he carried word of his findings to Dusty the better for the peace of the Backsight area. At which point Waco remembered the prisoner and knew he could not leave without her. Just as he decided to wait until after dark, he learned something which changed his mind. The rest of the hands, scattered in small groups vent-branding stock, would be returning by nightfall and if he aimed to make a move, he must do it quickly or have no chance at all. Given surprise, Waco reckoned he could handle the men present, but a larger number would be too much for him.

"Where's a man go, when he wants to go?" he asked.

"Out back. That's our'n in the open. The one in the hollow's where the boss ladies go."

Rising, Waco slouched across the room and went out of the side door. He had not removed his gunbelt and the Winchester rode the boot of his saddle down by the corral, so he possessed the armament he required. Leaving the building, he circled around and made for the house. On his arrival, he slipped along the porch, reached the front door and tried it. Much to his relief, the door opened and he looked inside cautiously. The hall was deserted and Waco cat-footed across towards the stairs.

"Hey, Joe," said a voice. "Where you go?"

Turning, Waco found a Chinese servant approaching him. Ever since meeting Tommy Okasi in the Rio Hondo, Waco had developed respect for the Oriental as a fighting man. While not knowing if all yellow-skinned men possessed Tommy's knowledge of unarmed combat, Waco reckoned that the present would be a mighty bad time to start finding out.

"Where's the boss lady?" he asked, standing innocently relaxed.

The Chinese servant saw nothing out of the ordinary in either the question or Waco's attitude. Having seen the way the sisters acted with Donglar, the servant could imagine why Waco came to the house and headed for the stairs. Although the man spoke little English, he understood Waco's question and knew how to make an answer. Suspecting nothing, he turned his pig-tailed head towards the dining-room door.

Down dipped Waco's left hand, hooking the near-side Colt from leather and bouncing its barrel off the Chinaman's head. Even as the man started to collapse, Waco caught him, supporting him and looking around for somewhere to conceal the unconscious form. Guessing that the door under the staircase opened into a broom closet, Waco hauled his burden to it. On opening the door, he found his guess correct and also that a piece of luck had come his way. In addition to cleaning materials, a coiled rope lay on the floor of the closet and with it Waco secured his victim. After using a piece of rag for a gag, Waco left the closet, closed its door behind him and went up the stairs without further interruption. With something like relief, he saw the key still in the door to Louise's prison room.

Louise Ortega sat on the bed, but she came to her feet, face showing apprehension and little fists clenched, as Waco entered.

"Don't make any fuss, ma'am!" he said urgently. "I've come to take you out of here."

"I——"

"This's no time to argue."

"How do I know I can trust you?" Louise asked. "You helped capture me."

"I had to," Waco answered. "But I work for Dusty Fog."

Seeing the disbelief which came to Louise's face, Waco thought fast in an attempt to find a way of proving he spoke the truth. He knew much about Dusty, Mark and the Kid and sought for the thing most likely to convince the girl of his *bona fides*. Few people would be expected to know that the Kid called his white stallion Blackie, but that was not conclusive. Several stories of Mark Counter's fantastic feats of strength—such as how he lifted the end of Calamity Jane's wagon out of a gopher hole,* or with his bare hands broke the neck of a longhorn bull†—came to mind, to be discarded as belonging to public knowledge. On her arrival in Backsight, Louise had so far forgotten her Southern lady's upbringing, due to a variety of circumstances, that she tangled in a hair-yanking brawl with her husband's sister; but many people knew of the incident.

Then Waco recalled something, an incident the true facts of which were known to not more than half-a-dozen people, Louise included.

"Mind the time when the Apaches jumped your train, ma'am?" he asked.

"Yes," she replied, wanting to believe him and wondering if he knew the right answer. "The Ysabel Kid ended it when he shot their chief——"

"Only it was Thad Baylor who did the shooting from inside your wagon. Lon went with him and came out holding the rifle so nobody'd tie Thad in with it."

No longer did disbelief show on the girl's face, for she knew Waco told her the truth. Only a real close friend of

*Told in *Troubled Range*. †Told in *The Man from Texas*.

Dusty Fog would have access to the information he gave her. In the War Between The States, Thad Baylor served as a sharp-shooter, as the special duty snipers of the period were called. A skilled gunsmith, he hated killing, yet found himself forced to take man after man's life. Even after the war Baylor found no respite, for law enforcement officers called him in to deal with situations where accurate shooting was necessary. At last, tired of being required to bring death from long ranges, Baylor decided to move West and make a fresh start. Under the name of Cauldon, he joined the Raines's wagon train as a gunsmith. During the Apache attack, the Kid saw a means of saving the train. An earlier failure caused the Indian leader to make fresh medicine and the Kid saw him at his prayers. If the chief died, the rest would go—but there was one small snag, he stood over five hundred yards away and beyond the range where the Kid's Winchester could make a hit. So Dusty asked Baylor, or Cauldon, to help and, to preserve his secret, arranged things so it appeared that the Kid did the shooting. In their relief at seeing the end of the attack, none of the travellers wondered how the Kid managed to make a hit at such a long range while using an unfamiliar rifle.

Only the Texans, Louise and her father, and Cauldon knew the true story of what happened in the Raines's wagon that day. If the tall young Texan knew the true facts, and clearly he did, he must be more than a mere employee on the O.D. Connected and trusted by Dusty Fog.

"I believe you," she said. "And I'm sorry——"

"Shucks, ma'am," grinned Waco. "Most folks start off by dang nigh scalping me bare-handed. You couldn't know how things stood. I had to stop you, or that big gal'd've done it with a gun. Reckon she's the Considine gal Dusty's told me about?"

"Yes. I knew she had broken out of prison, but thought she'd fled the country. Perhaps you'd better let me stay here——"

"No, ma'am. Not with what she has in mind for you.

Let's get going. We'll sneak out of here, grab a couple of hosses and make a run for either town or your place, whichever's nearer."

"All right," Louise breathed.

Cautiously Waco eased open the room door and looked along the passage. He then led the girl out and down the stairs.

"If we run into trouble," he whispered. "Head for the corral and leave me handle it."

"There's a side door through that room," Louise replied, indicating one of the doors leading off the main hall. "Terry and I came over here to look around just after we were married."

"We'll go out that way then. Sure hope there's nobody in the room though."

Gun in hand ready for use, Waco eased the door open and stepped into the room to find it deserted. With the girl on his heels, he walked across to the side door and let himself out of the house. Although the bunkhouse stood to one side, none of its occupants witnessed the departure and Waco decided that their luck held good. He concluded that they had best not press their good fortune.

"We'll cut around the back of the house and come in from the other side to the corral," he said and Louise followed without a word.

Just as they reached the end of the house, trouble struck. One of the hired guns had been in the backhouse attending to his normal functions and he chose that minute to come out. For a moment he stood staring at Louise and Waco, then he jerked the gun from the holster of his belt, which he carried in his hand, at the same time opening his mouth and yelling.

"Hey! What're you doing with that gal?"

"Eloping," Waco answered as the man fired at him.

The man shot from waist high, but his bullet came nowhere near Waco or the girl. Shooting by instinctive alignment could produce man-killing accuracy—but only at close range, and the gunhand stood a good fifty yards away. Up swung Waco's Colt, for the man blocked their escape and might improve his aim. There had been a time when Waco would have replied in the same manner that his assailant employed, throwing lead from waist level; but not since joining Dusty Fog and learning from a master how to make the most of his revolvers. The extra split-second necessary to extend the hand shoulder high and take sight proved their worth. On the crack of Waco's Colt, the hired gun jerked, spun around, dropped his revolver and fell sprawling into the backhouse.

Fast though Waco moved, the mischief had been done. The man's shout and shot, although they did not reach the sisters in the dining-room, alerted the rest of the ranch crew.

"Damn the luck!" Waco spat out. "Run for it, ma'am!"

Shouts sounded from the bunkhouse and feet thudded. Waco heard the door crash open. He threw two shots which kicked splinters from the wall and prevented the men from showing themselves. Whirling on his heels, the young Texan started after Louise. Ahead of the girl, the ranch's Chinese cook burst into sight at the end of the house. Brandishing a meat cleaver, he rushed forward at Louise. Waco fired, driving a bullet into the cook's chest and the man reeled backwards under the impact of the lead.

Ignoring the fallen man, Louise ran by the end of the house and Waco caught up with her. There would be no chance of making for the corral, so Waco headed the girl in the direction of the rough, broken country behind the buildings. Once there, he figured that he could make things mighty interesting for anybody who came after him. With the girl present, he might be hampered but knew he had one advantage over his pursuers. Spread out among the bush-dotted, rock-covered draws and valleys behind the house, they would have to make sure before they shot whether it was a friend or enemy. As long as Waco kept the girl at his side, he need be hampered by no fear of putting lead into a friend. Knowing hired guns, and having formed a pretty fair estimation of the quality of the Whangdoodle's crew, he reckoned he ought to be able to dissuade them. After that—well, much as he hated walking, Waco reckoned he could manage to hike overland to either Backsight or the Ortega place.

A few scattered shots followed the running pair, but they had already built up a fair lead and none of the bullets came close enough to worry them. Behind them, they heard Anthea yelling orders to the crew. Then they reached the mouth of a winding valley and entered it. Once out of sight of the ranch, Waco looked around for some way to throw the pursuit from their track.

"Agh!" Louise cried, her foot catching between two rocks. She fell forward and felt pain knife into her ankle.

"Can you walk?" Waco asked, dropping to one knee by her and looking back.

"I—I'll try," she replied, but on attempting to rise knew the awful truth. "I—I've sprained my ankle. Go without me."

"Like hell," he answered. "Hook your arm around my neck and hang on."

Before the girl could raise the objections which rose inside her, Waco bent down and scooped her into his arms. She hung on to his neck and he started to walk fast, swinging through the bushes and along a draw which ran at an angle to the valley he first entered. After quick thought, he decided to keep moving and chance being seen. To hole up would be of no use. The men could pin him down, fetch rifles from the house, or just wait until the full crew arrived and then take him by sheer weight of numbers. Gritting his teeth at the thought, Waco kept moving.

In that kind of deadly game, local knowledge could spell the difference between life and death. While Waco might be a stranger to the area, the same applied to all but one of his hunters. After Fernandez's death and the departure of his employees, Billy had spent a fair amount of time around the ranch, hunting jack-rabbits over the area into which Louise and Waco fled. Using his memory of the lie of the land, Billy guessed at which direction the Texan would go, and saw a chance of taking revenge on the man who rough-handled him.

"Come on," he said to the cowhand Waco had dumped into the water-trough. "You and me'll go off this way."

Fanned out in extended line, the ranch's crew headed for the broken ground. They advanced with caution, guessing that any lack of it while dealing with the gun-handy Texan was likely to prove fatal. Anthea watched her men as they moved off to disappear into the rough country. Without a word or glance at her sister, she started after the men. Face still twisted in lines of hatred, Myra followed Anthea at a short distance behind and made no attempt to catch up.

Keeping to cover as much as possible, Waco strode along with the girl in his arms. Once he froze as a member of the ranch crew appeared on a distant rim, but the man turned away without seeing them. Sliding down into the bottom of another draw, the Texan continued to move on. Waco concentrated his attention on keeping his sense of direction. In that kind of country, a man might easily become confused and wind up returning in the direction from which he came.

Noises beyond the rim of the draw brought Waco to a halt. Close at hand grew a clump of mesquite; poor cover, but all available right then. Swiftly Waco moved behind the bushes, lowered the girl and sank down by her side. Almost as soon as they hid, the girl and Waco saw a pair of men top the rim and look back along the draw. So far the men, members of a party who returned while Waco was at the house, scanned the draw to the rear of the hidden pair, but it would only be seconds before their scrutiny reached the mesquite which offered such scanty cover. Although Waco drew his gun, he did not cock it in case the sound drew the searchers' eyes to his position.

Away to the right of where Waco hid, one of the search-

ing pairs—the men decided, without discussion, to work
in twos rather than go up against the Texan singly—heard
a crashing in the bushes. Whirling, they brought up their
guns and fired in the direction of the sound before either
realised that their target was a whitetail deer buck that had
been sleeping the day in cover and disturbed by their presence. Not far away, another pair saw the movement of the
buck and joined in the bombardment and yet a third duo,
nerves on edge, added their quota to the shooting.

"Over there!" one of the pair above Waco yelled, turning
and bounding away.

Listening to the sounds of the men's departure, Waco
let out his breath in a low sigh of relief.

"Do I look any older?" he asked the girl, standing up
and helping her rise.

"No," she smiled.

"I sure feel it," Waco grinned and lifted Louise into his
arms ready to move on again.

At that moment Waco became aware of a fresh sound.
Hooves drummed ahead of them somewhere, although as
yet the riders had not come into sight. The sound gave the
youngster small comfort. Any riders in the area were almost
sure to be members of the Whangdoodle crew.

Ahead the draw widened out, its bottom fairly clear,
although the sides had a fair sprinkling of bushes and rocks
on them. Normally Waco would have swung away from
such an area, but he wanted to cross if only to find suitable
cover from which to make a stand. Carefully scanning the
sides of the draw, he walked forward.

"I wonder what they were shooting at," Louise whispered.

"Hope it was each other," Waco replied, "Happen
they——"

A shot crashed from up the side of the draw and slightly
behind Waco. Pain ripped into him, a cruel, burning agony
which tumbled him forward and caused him to drop the

girl. Even as Louise's horse-riding skill came into play and broke her fall, she twisted around and saw Waco sprawling on his right side. Beyond the stricken Texan, Billy and his companion rose from the bushes where they had hidden on seeing Waco's approach. Grinning at each other, they started down the slope. With the Texan either dead or badly injured, they expected no further trouble. The hooves came closer and Billy wanted to reach his victim before any other member of the crew arrived to share the credit.

Although the two young men thought they had an easy task on their hands, with Waco wounded and helpless, they reckoned without the courage and spirit of the girl. Louise Ortega came from a race of fighters, the kind who did not mildly let anyone abuse them. Reaching forward, she jerked Waco's left side Colt from its holster. With the gun gripped in both hands, Louise swung it up and lined it. Flame lashed from the five-and-a-half-inch barrel and Billy's companion reeled backwards, face a mask of blood.

Even as Billy sprang forward, he saw the Colt turn his way, its hammer drawing back under the girl's thumb. Cold fear ripped into him, but he could not halt his advance. Louise squeezed the trigger, but only a dry click rewarded her. Back at the ranch, Waco had fired off four shots from the Colt and followed the safety precaution of carrying his revolvers with an empty chamber under the hammer. Nor could Louise lay hands on the fully loaded right-side Colt, for Waco lay on it and pinned it to the ground.

Ignoring the thunder of approaching hooves, Billy walked forward. He saw from the weak movements that Waco was only wounded and decided to finish the Texan off before dealing with the girl. Leering sadistically, the young man halted, feet braced apart. While Louise desperately tried to free Waco's second revolver, Billy lined his gun down at the helpless form of the young Texan.

CHAPTER FIFTEEN

I Helped Design The First Of Them

Entering the Bismai Cafe. Backsight's Wells Fargo tele-graph operator looked across the room to where Dusty Fog, Mark Counter and Doc Leroy sat eating a late breakfast. Crossing to the Texans' table, he held out a buff-coloured message form to Dusty.

"This just came in from Yuma, Cap'n," he said. "Figured you'd want it now."

"Thanks," Dusty answered and read the message.

"Will there be any answer?" the man asked.

"Not right now," replied Dusty, passing the paper to Mark.

"It could be Baxter," Mark commented, after reading the answer to Dusty's message of the previous night. "Or a couple of dozen other fellers."

"What do you aim to do about it, Dusty?" Doc inquired when he had read the description of the man who engineered Anthea Considine's escape and compared it with the ap-pearance of Baxter, the saloon-keeper.

"I reckon we'll go to the Alamo and let Baxter settle it for us," Dusty said quietly.

Having seen the arrival of the operator, and guessed at his mission, Maisie deserted the cash desk and joined the

Texans. She took and read the message, thinking how inconclusive it was, then her eyes went to Dusty as he stood up.

"You're going to see him?"

"I reckon so."

"Can I do anything?"

"Not yet," Dusty answered. "Happen there's a whole heap of shooting, you can get some of the townsmen to lend us a hand. I hope it doesn't come to that, but it might."

"I'll see to it," Maisie promised.

Despite the easy manner in which he discarded the idea of trouble, Dusty knew the danger which lay ahead. "Baxter" had men to back him and, given an opportunity, a good place from which to make a fight. Like most buildings in town, especially those erected in the days before the Raines's train arrived, the Alamo had been strongly built to withstand visits by marauding Apaches. The saloon's walls would just as easily hold off the law enforcement officers in the event of a fight.

Another point Dusty kept constantly in mind. While the description could fit "Baxter," it also covered a number of other men for it had only general terms. So the Texans could not burst into the saloon painted for war, but must enter the Alamo with guns holstered and play the game as the cards fell.

Just as the three Texans left the eating house, they saw a rider approaching. Sudden apprehension bit into each of the trio as he recognised the Ysabel Kid, riding alone and leading four horses including an exceptionally fine paint stallion. For all his relief at the sight of a useful addition to his fighting strength, Dusty felt anxiety as he watched the trail dirty, gaunt, unshaven Kid bring the horses to a halt.

"Where's the boy?" Mark asked.

"Went over to Fernandez's old place to see what he could learn," the Kid answered, swinging from the saddle of his mount. "We heard that somebody was hiring guns up this way and reckoned the new owner out there'd be the most likely. So the boy went over to see if he could get hisself hired."

"He'll be all right, as long as he uses his head," Dusty said.

"Trust the boy for that," Doc went on.

"You going some place, Dusty?" the Kid inquired.

"To the Alamo. After we've tended to our business there, we might be riding to the Whangdoodle."

"If the boy's there, we'll have to move easy," Doc remarked, helping the Kid secure the horses.

"That figgers," answered Dusty. "What've you been doing, Lon?"

While drawing his rifle and accompanying the others along the street, the Kid quickly told of his actions after leaving them. Knowing the need, he went into detail of the more important visits made in the search for the man who placed the bounty on Dusty's head. By the time they reached the doors of the saloon, Dusty felt sure that he guessed correctly and "Baxter" was the man he wanted.

Crossing the sidewalk, Dusty led the way into the saloon. At that early hour only a few of the visiting hired guns and members of the saloon's staff were present, scattered about the room. All eyes went to the Texans and silence dropped among its occupants.

At the bar, where he stood checking a list of supplies, Donglar laid aside his pencil and stiffened slightly. A signal brought Edwards to his side and alerted the rest of the room to be ready for trouble. Outwardly it might have been a normal casual visit by the town's peace officers to a saloon, but Donglar's every instinct warned him of impending danger. For all that, Donglar gave no hint of his concern as Dusty and Mark walked towards him; even though he read a certain significance in the way the other two Texans remained standing on either side of the main entrance.

"What's this, Captain Fog?" Donglar asked cheerfully. "A social call, or another check on my gambling games?"

"Neither, Mr. Baxter—Or should I say 'Father Donglar?'"

"I don't follow you, Captain," Donglar purred, but he did.

"About that bounty *you* put on my scalp, mister," Dusty said in a carrying voice. "Do you have the guts to try for it yourself?"

Now Dusty had the attention of every man in the room. The hired guns knew of the reward, although none of them cared to take the risk of trying to collect it, and wondered if the small Texan told the truth when he claimed the saloon-keeper sent out the wanted posters. Behind the bar, Geordie—still smarting under his defeat at Dusty's hands, gave a glance at the sawed-off ten gauge which lay on the shelf beneath the counter. Casually Geordie inched along to where he could reach down and grab the deadly weapon.

"You've gone way past me now, Fog," Donglar stated.

"And you're a liar," Dusty drawled, but Donglar did not make the expected reply to the supreme insult of the West.

"You started the dodgers from Pasear Hennessey's place and the man who collected had to go there. When he got there, he was to be sent to Dougal's, then on to Frenchy Latour's saloon—Only I don't need to go on, do I?"

Even as he listened, Donglar knew he must fight for his life. If the Texan knew so much, he had enough evidence to make an arrest. Once held, Donglar knew it would be an easy matter to have the Warden from Yuma come over and identify him. However, Donglar did not make his move immediately. All too well he knew the fear Dusty Fog's reputation inspired among his men. They would not back their boss in a fight while the deadly Rio Hondo gun-wizard lived. If Donglar expected help, he must take Dusty Fog out of the game.

On four occasions during the past three years, a similar

situation faced Donglar and he could guess how the men before him would react. He wore his gun, but still in that high and awkward-looking holster. As before, it seemed that the Texans disregarded Donglar as a factor; confining their attention to Edwards, who wore his weapon in a conventional rig the potentiality of which they readily understood. If Dusty Fog died, his friends were likely to be frozen by shock for the vital moment necessary to enable the saloon crowd to get into action. It only remained for somebody to supply the necessary ingredient to bring the whole pot to a satisfactory, from Donglar's point of view, boil.

"You wouldn't be trying to push me out for Eddy Last, now would you?" Donglar asked, setting up an excuse for defending his property.

"You know I'm not. I'm arresting you for assisting a prisoner to escape from the Territorial Penitentiary," Dusty answered, then went on with an additional charge brought out by a piece of information in the telegraph message. "They found the two old men you killed, so I want you for murder, too. And then there's the attempted murder of Town Marshal Randel right here in Backsight."

"My my!" Donglar sneered. "Haven't I been a bad boy? Do you think you can make any of the charges stick?"

"I aim to have a try."

"You'll have to take me first," Donglar pointed out.

"Which shouldn't raise me any sweat at all," Dusty answered.

"You've taken it, Fog!" Donglar thought and made his move.

Dropping his right shoulder slightly caused Donglar's coat side to swing away from his body. Around circled his right hand in a lightning fast move aimed to draw the Merwin and Hulbert revolver from that awkward-appearing—but ideally placed for use with a short-barrelled weapon—holster.

On each other occasion when Donglar found need to

throw down on a man, his speed from the apparently wrongly-placed rig took his victim by surprise. Too late he saw the error of his thinking and realised that Dusty had not disregarded him as a dangerous factor in the game.

An instant after Donglar's shoulder began its preliminary move, Dusty's left hand crossed to the white butt of the right side Colt and slid it from leather. Even so, fast as he moved, Dusty would have died had he been using a lighter, less powerful weapon. Donglar's gun was out and swinging up into line, its hammer drawing back, when two hundred and fifty grains of lead tore into his body and the agonizing shock threw him backwards. Incredulity mingled with the pain on Donglar's face as his numbed fingers opened and allowed the gun to drop, then he went to the floor.

Part of Donglar's conclusions had been correct. Mark's attention stayed on Edwards, for the blond giant left Dusty to handle the saloon-keeper. Since seeing the speed of Mark's draw, Edwards had given much thought to whether his own speed exceeded that of the big Texan's. His question received its answer as his gun cleared leather, for a bullet from Mark's right hand Colt drove between the gambler's eyes and tumbled him lifeless to land at his boss's side.

The opening moves in the deadly affair came so fast and unexpected that none of the crowd fully understood until too late what was happening. In a way, Donglar's draw took his men unprepared for none could say how well he might handle a gun. Geordie recovered first among the saloon employees. Dipping down his hands, he started to bring the shotgun over the bar. Across the room, the Kid's rifle flowed to his shoulder, lined and spat, its lever blurring to replace the expended round with a loaded bullet. With the shotgun lifting, the Kid shot the only way he dared. Striking Geordie between the eyes, the bullet passed through his head, bursting out at the rear and shattering a bottle on the shelf behind him.

"Down!" Doc snarled, his Colt flickering out to line on Geordie's friends.

Only half-rose and with hands far from their guns, Preston and Dink sank down once again. They had witnessed the speed with which Doc drew and knew that such ability only rarely went without an equal skill at planting home lead with accuracy.

"Anybody else want to take it up for Baxter?" asked Dusty, his left-hand Colt augmented by the right, both making an arc around the room.

Silence fell, not even a loud breath breaking it, after Dusty issued his challenge. Seeing their boss stretched out on the floor, the saloon's staff knew they had nothing to fight for. The same applied to the hired guns, only even more so, for Donglar had not hired any of them and they fought only when paid to do so.

Moving slowly, Donglar raised himself from the floor, a hand pressed to the wound. He knew he must be dying, yet wanted to learn how he came to fail to take Dusty by surprise.

"You—knew about—my holster," he gasped, looking at the small Texan. "But I didn't think anybody in the West had seen one."

"I helped design the first of them," Dusty replied and motioned Doc Leroy forward.

In the days when Lieutenant Ballinger of the Chicago Police Department learned how to fight with a gun, Dusty acted as tutor and after much experimentation produced an identical holster to the one worn by Donglar. While the holster found favor among Eastern detectives, who required to hide their weapon under a jacket, men out West preferred the traditional pattern. Seeing a detective's holster while visiting Chicago, Donglar recognised its potential and went to the trouble of mastering its use. Until he met Dusty Fog, no man who faced him realised the danger such a rig presented—until too late.

Doc needed only one glance to know nothing he could do would save Donglar. In fact Doc felt surprised that the man had sufficient strength to ask the question. Even as

Doc began to kneel ready to do the little he could, Donglar's eyes glazed over and he sank back to the floor.

"It's over, Dusty," Doc said, straightening after closing Donglar's eyes.

"Like you say, Doc," Dusty answered, "it's over." His eyes went to the hired guns who sat in strained attitudes around the room. "There's no work for you around here. The man who put the bounty on my head is dead."

"Spread the word when you leave," Mark went on. "And leave before nightfall, every last son of you."

"We'll be around to see any one who don't leave," the Kid promised.

"How about us, Cap'n?" asked Preston.

"Your boss's dead. I'll ask the local judge to rule on what happens to the place."

"Sure," grunted Preston and rose. "We'll start cleaning up if we can."

"Get to it," Dusty confirmed and turned to leave the room followed by his three friends.

A small crowd of local men was gathering as the Texans emerged from the Alamo. Looking around, Dusty saw Thad Baylor approaching and when the gunsmith arrived said: "I had to kill Baxter inside."

"We all know that you had good reason to, Captain," Baylor replied and the crowd rumbled its agreement. "Can we do anything for you?"

"Sure. Go inside and take over until the law decides what to do with the place."

"How about Baxter's men?"

"I'll come in with you."

Although several of the saloon's employees had hoped to enrich themselves before leaving town, none raised any objections when Dusty told them that the gunsmith would act as manager until Baxter's affairs were settled. Already the hired guns finished their drinks and made for the doors, meaning to ride on in search of other employment.

Having disposed of the saloon problem temporarily, Dusty

rejoined the other three outside. Before any of them could say a word, they saw Maisie burst out of the Bismai, followed by a tall, freckled-faced, pleasant-looking young man in range clothing. All saw the expression on Maisie's face and expected trouble even before she reached them.

"It's Louise!" she said. "Terry here just came in. He says that she rode over to the Whangdoodle visiting."

"What's this all about, Dusty?" Terry Ortega demanded distractedly.

"The Considine woman's at the Whangdoodle," Dusty answered. "If Louise falls into her hands——"

"We'd best ride, and *pronto!*" Mark stated.

"You never said a truer word," Dusty replied.

"I'll need a hoss, Dusty," the Kid said. "Even Blackie's been pushed so hard that he'd slow you down."

"Come with me to the livery barn, Lon," Maisie ordered. "We'll get the best mounts it can offer."

"We?" asked Dusty.

"I'm coming along with you," the woman answered determinedly. "It was Baxter who shot Biscuits, wasn't it?"

"We didn't prove it, but it sure looks that way," Dusty agreed.

"Then he did it at her orders, which means I've a score to settle with her. Besides, you'll need a woman to handle her."

"Go get your gun, Maisie," Dusty ordered. "Terry, go with Lon, pick out and saddle the best three horses the barn can offer. And take it easy. One of my crew, you haven't met him, is out there. He'll see nothing happens to Louise."

Although Terry Ortega knew Dusty would not raise a false hope, he was in an understandable muck-sweat to get started. However, the Kid insisted that they leave nothing to chance, selecting the best horses, checking shoes and ensuring that all had their saddles and bridles fitted properly before going to join the others at the civic pound. While the men prepared the horses, Maisie changed into a shirt-waist and jeans. She joined the others, a Navy Colt thrust into her belt. People tended to regard the old percussion-fired revolvers as out-of-date, but every man present knew that, if the chips went down, Maisie could hold her own in a shooting fuss with that .36 caliber predecessor of the Peacemaker.

Mounting their horses, the grim-faced party rode from town. It was well for Maisie that she kept herself in practice by riding out regularly, for during the journey to the Whang-doodle she learned the kind of horsemanship which made Dusty's company of cavalry such masters of the riding arts. Alternating between a fast trot and walking alongside their mounts, they covered the miles at a speed that lesser men could not have accomplished without ruining the horses; and still retained a reserve of speed in the animals should it be needed.

While preparing to leave, Dusty forced Terry Ortega to be calm and give a detailed description of the Whangdoodle headquarters' layout. On the basis of what he learned, Dusty decided they would approach the ranch through the rough country behind the buildings and close in by stealth if possible, or a rush should it be necessary. With luck, Waco would be able to hold off harm from Louise and their arrival save her; or if they came too late—and none of them wished to think of that—avenge her.

Shooting reached their ears as they approached the ranch; too scattered for it to be target practice. Dusty wasted no time on speculation.

"Fan out and move!" he ordered. "Stick by me, Maisie!"

Swinging out into an extended line, the Texans, Ortega and Maisie sent their horses leaping forward at a better pace, utilizing the reserve of energy saved during the way out. Due to the broken nature of the country, the party soon lost sight of each other. Mark Counter tore along the bottom of a draw, heard two shots ahead of him. Rounding a bend, he saw something which caused him to urge his blood bay forward at a better pace.

CHAPTER SIXTEEN

A Little Knowledge

Standing over Waco's body, Billy slanted down his gun and ignored the approaching rider. Behind him, the ground shook to onrushing hooves. A low, almost animal in its savagery, snarl sounded and then a heavy body struck Billy with such force that it knocked him away from his victim and bore him to the ground. Fingers like steel clamped hold of the top of Billy's head, another hand gripping his shoulder in a numbing grasp. Then the upper hand twisted.

Louise had only a blurred impression of what happened. Even though she knew Mark—and had fallen mildly in love with him on the way out, although he never knew of it— the girl barely recognised the blond giant as he bore down on the would-be killer of her rescuer. She saw Billy knocked aside and down, heard the crash of his gun and saw dirt fly into the air inches away from Waco's body, and felt sure that her ears caught a dull popping noise.

Riding, his face twisted now in a look of anguish, Mark ran towards Waco, saw the youngster's body move and lifted his voice in a bull-like roar.

"Doc! Doc! Get here *pronto!* The boy's been shot!"

"I'm coming!" Doc's voice replied. "So're some of the Whangdoodle bunch."

"I'll tend to them!" Mark promised and ran to where his huge stallion stood waiting. Swinging into the saddle, he charged along the draw, pulling his guns as he went.

Staring around her, Louise finally looked at Billy. Something seemed wrong with the way the young cowhand lay. Not for a moment did the girl realise that while Billy's belly touched the ground his nose pointed straight up into the air.

Swinging his horse in the direction of Mark's voice, Doc sent it bounding recklessly over the rim and down into the draw. Almost as quickly, Maisie appeared at the other side. A gasp of relief left her lips as she saw Louise apparently unharmed, if pallid and shaken by her experiences. Maisie did not know Waco, although she had heard enough about him from the Texans, but she still felt a sudden anguish as she saw the youngster stretched out on the ground.

Doc wasted no time in dropping from his saddle and opening its pouch to take out a small roll of surgical instruments, some of them made to his own design, specially made for removing bullets. Ignoring the crash of shots which rolled in the background, he dropped to his knees by Waco's body and made a preliminary investigation. Swiftly he cut away the clothing from around the wound and looked down at it. Doc sucked in his breath as he studied the wound, for it was as bad as he had ever been called upon to handle.

"How can we help?" Maisie asked.

"Get your gun out and shoot any son who comes up, unless it's one of us," Doc answered and looked at Louise. "Take out your handkerchief, if you have one, or use your petticoat. Keep wiping the sweat away so it doesn't get into my eyes."

Although the sight of the wound sickened her, Louise nodded her head. While Maisie stood watch, her Navy Colt ready for use, Doc started the fight to save Waco's life, bringing in every bit of skill he possessed to play in a desperate race against time.

Separated from her men, Anthea Considine topped the

rim in almost the place from which Billy shot Waco down. Halting, she stared down into the draw and her lips drew back in a snarl of fury. From what she had seen and heard, her men were scattered and defeated, her plans for revenge ruined. Yet she might still wreak vengeance on at least one of her enemies. There below her stood the woman whose bullet tore into her arm and whose investigations provided the evidence which sent her to prison. Two horses stood in the draw, the means of escape she so badly needed. Lifting her Colt, she started to sight it at Maisie. First the woman, then that pallid cowhand working on the wounded Texan. With them dead, Anthea figured she could get the horses, take Louise as a hostage and run for safety.

For the first time since leaving the ranch, Myra managed to close up on her sister. Fury still bit at the girl, the blind rage which Anthea could usually keep under control ran in the family although Myra never managed to check her streak. Still smouldering from the memory of the blow Anthea landed on her, wild with jealousy, Myra came close behind her sister. The Derringer in her hand pressed against Anthea's spine and Myra's finger pressed on the trigger. Even as the gun bellowed, Myra thumbed back the hammer. The unmatched cogs of the operating ratchet caused the hammer to move down and on a second squeeze at the trigger, the lower barrel belched flame, sending its load into Anthea as she staggered forward.

At the foot of the draw, Maisie whirled towards the sound of the shots. She brought up her Navy as she saw Anthea Considine rear into sight on top of the rim. Before Maisie could fire, she saw the agony on the woman's face. Slowly Anthea opened her right hand, the Colt dropping from it. Then her legs buckled and she fell forward, sliding down the slope until stopped by a bush.

Maisie saw Myra's head turn and start to move away. Already the shooting had faded off into the background and Maisie doubted if there would be any danger to Doc or

Waco from the Whangdoodle crew. One thing was for sure. That girl on the rim must not be allowed to escape. Unless Maisie missed her guess, the girl had been "Baxter's" accomplice in freeing Anthea Considine. For the future peace of Backsight, she must be captured.

Darting up the slope, Maisie paused for a moment to look at Anthea. One glance told Maisie that she needed waste no time on the woman. Either of the bullets would have proved fatal. Cautiously Maisie topped the rise. Anthea had been a good shot and unafraid of using a gun, so Maisie took no chances when dealing with a woman whose facial resemblance hinted at being Considine's sister.

The cautions proved needless. On topping the rim, Maisie saw Myra running along the slope at a fair speed and making no attempt to stop or fight. Bringing up her Navy, Maisie yelled for the other to stop, and when the order was ignored fired a shot. At that range a hit would have been more luck than skilled aim, but for all that the bullet passed close enough to Myra's head to hand her a nasty shock. It did not, however, cause her to slacken her speed.

Without wasting any more lead, Maisie took up the chase; but the younger woman drew ahead and passed out of sight over a slope. Sliding down the other side, Myra staggered across the bottom. Her breath came in choking gasps, for she was scared and unused to such strenuous exercise. Ahead lay a clump of bushes and the girl threw herself among them, crouching down like a terrified, weasel-hunted rabbit. Managing to control her breathing, she peered back through the bushes and saw Maisie appear on top of the slope. For a moment Maisie stood looking around, then started downwards in the direction of the bushes.

Cold fear ran through Myra as she watched the grim-faced little woman come closer. Myra suddenly remembered that Maisie had been the one who shot her sister and recollected the times Anthea cursed the other's skill with a gun. If Maisie once saw Myra—the girl shuddered at the thought. Then another thought hit her, one which bit through her fear and roused a primeval instinct for self-preservation. The gun in her hand was empty.

Unlike her sister, Myra had little knowledge of weapons. She had seen both Anthea and Donglar load the Derringer, but in her arrogant way never asked to be shown how to do it. Gripping the barrels of the gun in her left hand, she fumbled for, found and pressed the catch, then broke open the gun. Still holding the gun in her left hand, its barrels pointing towards her body, she drew out the empty cases with her right forefinger and thumb, replacing them with loaded bullets.

Looking through the bushes, Myra found to her horror that Maisie had reached the foot of the slope and advanced towards the bushes. Panic hit the girl. Grabbing down, she gripped the butt of the gun in her right hand. Being right-handed, Myra tended to use it more than her left, especially when acting instinctively. So it proved in that instance. Wanting to have the weapon ready for use, she jerked the butt upwards to close the action. Not having learned the correct way of handling the gun, Myra did not know of its deadly effect. The hammer, down after firing the second shot, drove home on to the rim of the lower cartridge. Flame ripped from the muzzle of the gun. Burning agony knifed into Myra's body as the .41 bullet tore into her stomach. Myra screamed, rearing up into sight. Tense and ready for trouble, Maisie reacted instinctively. Bringing up her Navy, she fired once and this time did not miss. On moving forward, she parted the bushes and approached where Myra lay sprawled on the ground. After picking up the Derringer and setting it at half-cock, Maise returned her Colt to her waistband and knelt by the girl. A doctor might have saved Myra—but the only medical aid within many miles worked at extracting a bullet from the body of his best friend.

Hooves sounded and Dusty rode up, dropping from his paint, then joining Maisie in the bushes.

"I heard the shot and fired back," Maisie said, pallid of face, as she did what she could for the dying girl.

"You couldn't have known what happened," Dusty replied, glancing down at the Derringer and guessing how Myra received her first wound. "How's the boy?"

"I don't know. You'd best go and find out."

By the time Dusty reached the draw, he found Mark and the Kid waiting. Below them Terry Ortega held Louise in his arms and Doc rose, his face haggard, from the side of the still shape on the ground. Mark, his hat holed by a bullet, turned a strained face towards Dusty. Standing at Dusty's other side, even the Kid's impassive features showed concern. They had fought a bloody little battle with the Whangdoodle crew and five more bodies scattered in the broken country before the rest broke and ran. Now they gathered to learn whether the boy would live.

At last Dusty started to walk down the slope towards Doc. It took an effort, but the small Texan managed at last to say, "How is he, Doc?"

For a moment Doc did not reply, but his face showed plainly the strain of anxiety he had been under. Finally Doc smiled weakly and replied, "He'll live, Dusty. But it'll be a fair piece before he rides again."

WANTED:
Hard Drivin' Westerns From

J.T.Edson

J.T. Edson's famous "Floating Outfit"
adventure books are on every Western fan's
MOST WANTED list. Don't miss <u>any</u> of them!

___	THE COLT AND THE SABRE	09341-7/$2.50
___	THE GENTLE GIANT	08974-6/$2.50
___	GO BACK TO HELL	09101-5/$2.50
___	HELL IN THE PALO DORO	09361-1/$2.50
___	THE HIDE AND TALLOW MEN	08744-1/$2.50
___	THE MAKING OF A LAWMAN	06841-2/$2.25
___	OLD MOCCASINS ON THE TRAIL	08278-4/$2.50
___	THE QUEST FOR BOWIE'S BLADE	09113-9/$2.50
___	RETURN TO BACKSIGHT	09397-2/$2.50
___	SET TEXAS BACK ON HER FEET	08651-8/$2.50
___	THE TEXAS ASSASSIN	09348-4/$2.50
___	THE TRIGGER MASTER	09087-6/$2.50
___	WACO'S DEBT	08528-7/$2.50
___	THE YSABEL KID	08393-4/$2.50

★★★★★★★★★★★★★★★★★★

The Biggest, Boldest, Fastest-Selling Titles in Western Adventure!

★★★★★★★★★★★★★★★★★★

CHARTER'S MOST WANTED LIST

Merle Constiner

_81721-1 TOP GUN FROM THE DAKOTAS — $2.50

_24927-2 THE FOURTH GUNMAN — $2.50

Giles A. Lutz

_34286-8 THE HONYOCKER — $2.50

_88852-6 THE WILD QUARRY — $2.50

Will C. Knott

_29758-7 THE GOLDEN MOUNTAIN — $2.25

_71147-2 RED SKIES OVER WYOMING — $2.25

Benjamin Capps

_74920-8 SAM CHANCE — $2.50

_82139-1 THE TRAIL TO OGALLALA — $2.50

_88549-7 THE WHITE MAN'S ROAD — $2.50
